"Did you see anyone in the area after your sighting?" the government agent pressed.

Derek took a deep breath as he thought back on that night. No one else had been there. Except Kristiana.

His stomach flipped. How had she gotten there? Where had she come from?

Suddenly dizzy, he shook his head in disbelief. What he was thinking wasn't possible.

If Kristiana was... If these men found out about her...

Silently releasing the air from his lungs, Derek turned his back on the agents to stare out the window and hide the impact of the revelation. Kristiana wasn't from Earth! She was an alien! And he was in love with her.

ABOUT THE AUTHOR

Having a vivid imagination, Kim Hansen has always been intrigued by the possibilities offered through scientific exploration—whether it be in outer space, in the sea or in her own backyard where she can study the stars, the flowers or watch her two cats, Squirt and Small Fry, play. This is her second American Romance novel.

Books by Kim Hansen

HARLEQUIN AMERICAN ROMANCE
548—TIME RAMBLER

Kim Hansen

CLOSE ENCOUNTER

Harlequin Books

TORONTO • NEW YORK • LONDON
AMSTERDAM • PARIS • SYDNEY • HAMBURG
STOCKHOLM • ATHENS • TOKYO • MILAN
MADRID • WARSAW • BUDAPEST • AUCKLAND

To stargazers everywhere—
remember, there are always possibilities

ISBN 0-373-16604-4

CLOSE ENCOUNTER

Chapter One

What was wrong? Alarms were ringing, gauges were whirling, and the panels were masses of blinking lights. Some were flashing red, others amber, but all meant one thing: her ship was out of control.

Kristiana struggled to stay upright in her seat as the small spacecraft she was piloting plummeted madly through the black void. All the instruments were telling her the ship had suffered a major malfunction. The engines were misfiring, the fuel was ejecting, and the helm and navigational systems were no longer consistently responding to her commands.

As she fought to regain control, a frown lined her face and the light blue of her eyes darkened with fear. She couldn't understand what might have happened, and she had no time to figure it out. With life support and all other systems failing, her sole concern would be survival. She had to try to land the craft on the nearest planet and pray that a rescue ship would find her quickly.

Gritting her teeth against the violent shaking of the vessel, she reached out and punched the shiny red button on the far side of the main control panel. In all her years of space travel, she'd never had to use it. But then, she'd never been in an emergency situation before, either.

A bright green light blinked on. The distress beacon was on its way. It was impossible to guess how long it would be before her cry for help was heard by the mother ship she had been on her way to rejoin, but when it was received, her call would precipitate an immediate rescue launch. Her companions would rush to interpret the signal detailing her present coordinates, the condition of her ship, and what she was about to attempt: landing on an alien planet.

Already the gravity of the third planet from the sun had caught her ship and was pulling her toward it at a frightening speed. During an ordinary approach, she would have enjoyed the beauty of the glittering blue orb. But as she struggled with the damaged spacecraft, she had no time to appreciate anything about the world called Earth by its inhabitants. Still, at least she knew something of the planet and its people. She had visited it before and, if necessary, she could live among its inhabitants for the short time she hoped it would take her friends to answer the beacon.

Resisting the panic bubbling in her throat, Kristiana calmly sent her fingers flying over the control panel in an attempt to smoothly guide the shuddering craft into the Earth's atmosphere. She frowned when she saw that the screening mechanism had burned out. That meant her cloaking device wasn't working, and any watching eye—trained or untrained—on the planet below would see her coming. But, she could do nothing about it. When and if she landed safely, she only hoped to have enough time to destroy the ship and any other evidence of her presence before being discovered.

Blazing into the upper atmosphere at light speed, she ignored the whine of the engines, the flashing lights of the control panel, and the rising temperature in the cabin as the outside shields began to overheat. Sweat formed on her brow. She concentrated, instead, on finding a place to land.

The navigation controls were sluggish, but the helm was responding. She would be able to avoid any cities or other populated areas. And that was important. She had no wish to hurt anyone by her unexpected arrival.

Reducing speed and aiming for an open area where her sensors indicated no human life stood, Kristiana cut all power, bit her lip and prayed as the ground rushed upward.

A SHORT DISTANCE away from a deserted field, Derek Carpenter stood staring up at the night sky, his hands stuffed into the pockets of his gray slacks. It was a clear night over the state of Illinois and, far from the lights of the cities, a million stars could be seen shining above the earth. It was a beautiful, even peaceful sight, but it was one that had been disturbed only moments before.

Driving home in the dead of night, Derek had been alone on the highway when a streak of light appeared from nowhere to sear its way across the sky. Awe-struck, he'd watched silently as whatever it was lit up the countryside for miles around before disappearing abruptly over a hill on the horizon. A frown had curved his lips as he'd wondered if a meteor or a malfunc-tioned satellite had collided with Earth.

He sighed and turned from the mysterious unknown to the reality of the neon lights of the gas station he'd stopped at to fill up. Whatever the fiery missile had been, it was doubtful he'd ever hear anything more about it. The government was not fond of admitting something had invaded U.S. space, and they'd be particularly secretive if, indeed, one of their billion-dollar projects had just crashed into the dirt.

Pacing restlessly away from his car but remaining in the glow of the flashing sign that read Open 24 Hours For All Your Needs, Derek looked to be exactly what he was—a weary executive on his way home from a business trip. The usually immaculately pressed gray suit he wore was wrinkled from the passage of time and the effects of travel. The knot of the silk tie at his neck had been yanked down and hung at a crooked angle from the open collar of his creased white shirt. The shadow of a night's beard darkened his jaw as the gold watch on his wrist warned of one day's passing and another's start.

Shoving an impatient hand through his thick, dusty-blond hair, his hazel gaze swept the station grounds in search of the attendant who had disappeared inside several minutes ago to run a credit card payment through a computer. The young boy was nowhere in sight. Derek took a step toward the station door but stopped abruptly.

Why was he in such a hurry to be on his way? He had no place special to go, nothing to do, and no one to see. Only his empty house was waiting for him. And it was early Sunday morning. He could relax. The office wouldn't be open again until Monday. Indeed, instead of driving through the night to get home, he could have lounged around Indianapolis for the rest of the weekend. Yet the moment the Saturday afternoon meeting had ended, he'd gotten into his car and started the journey back.

Shaking his head, Derek walked back to his sleek four-door sedan and leaned against the front fender, fighting the driving urge that always had him moving, working, doing. But it was difficult. Staying busy had become a habit he couldn't break. A necessity at first, caused by the youthful need to prove himself, work had become a balm for grief when death had robbed him of his only family. Then work quickly became overwork that had carried him forward until staying active had become a way of life.

"Here you go, Mr. Carpenter," the attendant announced, reappearing to hurry across the lot with the credit card, a copy of the charge slip, and a big grin. "Have a nice day."

Derek managed to return the smile, temporarily banishing his brooding contemplation as he accepted the plastic and paper before stepping into his car. But his thoughts turned dark again as he put the key into the ignition and guided the sedan back out onto the lonely highway.

He seemed always to be rushing somewhere. Out of high school, he had raced into medical school, where he'd spent two years before realizing it wasn't for him. His dream of becoming a doctor who cured and healed had ended the day a man collapsed in front of him on a busy sidewalk and died because Derek hadn't had the medicine needed to keep the man's heart pumping.

Knowing that it was often a combination of people *and* drugs that saved lives, he'd rushed off to learn about pharmacology. The move had cost him not only a career but the woman he'd been engaged to marry. Valerie, his high school sweetheart, who had also chosen to follow the road to becoming a physician, hadn't understood his motives or been able to accept his willingness to let go of their dream to forge a partnership in both marriage and profession. Ironically, the career change had failed to appease his seemingly innate need to do some greater good.

He sighed. Looking back, it was difficult to understand how his parents had remained supportive through those trying years. But they had been supportive, and it was his successful businessman father who'd given him the challenge he needed—a loan to start his own company.

Steering the car around a curve at a smooth seventy miles an hour with silent ease, Derek frowned fiercely out the windshield. Even though that small beginning had mushroomed into a pharmaceutical conglomerate specializing in medical research, he couldn't shake the frustrating feeling that while he was rapidly approaching the age of thirty, he still hadn't reached that elusive goal he'd been striving for since enrolling in medical school years ago.

Pushing the gas pedal closer to the floor, he roared into another curve. The headlights cut through the black emptiness of night and suddenly pinned a deer standing in the middle of the road. Derek slammed on the brakes and swerved violently.

The tires squealed, the startled doe rushed off, and a muffled thud came from the rear seat. Swearing, Derek jerked the car to a complete halt. He barely felt something hit the back of his seat because he was already jumping out onto the road and yanking open the rear door.

His hand closed blindly over a collar, and he yanked someone from the car floor and outside into the night.

"What the hell are you doing here?"

His bellow had the person he'd grabbed cringing, and Derek's scowl deepened as he tried to determine in the dark if it was a man or a woman he held. The only illumination on the highway came from his headlights, the car's interior ceiling lamp, and the stars high above, but as shadowed eyes were tentatively raised to his, long, blond hair glinted in the night. A woman. His lips thinned.

"Who are you? And what are you doing in my car?"

She didn't answer. Silent, she merely stared up at him while trying to lean away from the heat of his fury.

Gritting his teeth, Derek glared at her in frustration. He couldn't make out her features clearly, but she was tall and slim and dressed all in black. The long, blond—almost white—hair was the only part of her that he could see well. "Where did you come from?"

With her arm trapped by hard fingers, and pinned by a menacing gaze, Kristiana struggled to find her tongue and an answer. Fortunately the language the man was using was familiar. She'd learned and even spoken it on a prior trip to the planet. But her mind was still reeling from the crash landing and her narrow escape.

It had been a rough landing and too close to a populated area. By the time she'd gotten out of the ship, the first Earthling had already been standing on top of a nearby hill. But she hadn't been able to run. The sealing of her craft had taken precedence over her own safety.

Destroying the entire ship would have been desirable but impossible without endangering those already rushing to the crash site. Her only option had been to set the self-destruct mechanism that would cause an explosion inside the vessel. Once the charge was detonated, the ship would collapse upon itself and thereby protect the technology within. Not every planet was ready for interstellar space travel. To leave clues on how to accomplish such voyages could put a people in astral space well before they were prepared for the possibility.

Even though she had engaged the self-destruct program before leaving the site, with the controls so badly damaged, she wondered whether the system had remained operational. The timer had beeped immediately upon activation, but she hadn't been able to stay to ensure the charge had detonated. With sirens whining and people shouting, she'd had to flee, hoping that no one would notice her escape. She'd hoped, too, that when the experts arrived to investigate the crash, the interior of the ship would be no more than a mass of melted metal and wire, and that its condition would lead all to believe that any crew had been killed on impact.

"I asked you a question."

Kristiana cringed again from the large man holding her so tightly. Unfortunately, surviving the landing and escaping immediate danger of discovery hadn't guaranteed her safety. Struggling to get as far away from the crash site as possible, the fueling station had been a blessing, the lone vehicle at the colorful pumps, a bonus. She had slipped inside, hoping to stay undetected long enough to achieve a sufficient amount of distance between her and the ship to guarantee safety until rescue could arrive. But now, facing the land vehicle's very angry owner, she suddenly doubted the wisdom of her plan. She pointed back down the road. "Gasoline..."

"You crawled into my car while I was getting gas?"

"Yes." Kristiana swallowed with difficulty. The man confronting her was very tall. He stood more than six feet tall, and the width of his shoulders evinced intimidating strength.

"Why?"

She opened her mouth to speak, but it was impossible to tell him that she was running from the Earth authorities. If only he hadn't swerved so unexpectedly.

Derek's lips thinned when she failed to respond. Her continued silence was annoying, but she was obviously afraid. It showed in the way she hung her head and in how she cringed from him. And, considering how he was yelling at her, he couldn't blame her. He smothered a sigh and tried to draw on what little patience he had, releasing her to drag a hand through his hair. "You don't look like a potential mugger so you must just be looking for a ride."

Kristiana's eyes lifted dubiously to his. Some of the anger had left his voice, and his tone meant more to her than his words. She might know his language, but it'd been a long time since she'd visited his planet and heard actual Earth speech.

"How many people turned you down before you decided to choose me with a do-it-yourself invitation?" In the dim light from the car, Derek saw a smudge on her cheek. "You certainly look dirty enough to have been at it for a while."

With no other good answer to provide, and struggling to follow the questions he asked so rapidly, Kristiana hastily agreed. "Yes."

"Why didn't you just ask?"

Her eyes fell from his.

"Thought you'd get turned down, is that it?"

"Yes." The word was little more than a mumble.

"You probably would have been."

"Yes."

Derek swore under his breath. "Is that all you can say? *Yes?*"

Kristiana flinched as the anger returned to his voice, and decided it would be prudent to leave him alone. She would have to find another way to escape the vicinity of the crash site. "I will go now. I am sorry to have..." She searched her memory for the proper words. "Disturbed you."

Derek watched in disbelief as she abruptly turned to walk away into the black of night and quickly reached out to catch her arm. "Wait a minute!"

Her cry of pain surprised them both, and he let go of her to see her grab her upper arm. "You're not dirty. You're hurt!"

Before Kristiana could object, she was caught again in his grip and pulled gently toward the light of the car.

Derek carefully peeled the torn, leatherlike material of her jumpsuit away from her upper arm to examine the wound beneath. It was red, bleeding and raw. Standing closer to her, he noticed the distinct smell of smoke. "How did this happen?"

"An accident."

He threw her a sharp look. Could she be in shock? It wouldn't be the first case where a victim had walked away from a car crash to wander around aimlessly, if seemingly coherently, before rational thought returned hours, or even days, later.

"I am fine," Kristiana managed to object at his startled stare. It was becoming a little easier to speak and grasp the English he was using, but her effort to back away from him was thwarted when he suddenly caught her jaw to stare into her eyes. She stilled, and was shocked when he reached out to brush the hair from her face before pushing his fingers into its mass to do a cursory examination of her skull.

"Did you hit your head?"

"No." His sudden physical contact made her breathless, and her heart leapt against her breast as she looked up to meet the cool, golden brown of his gaze. All of her people had blue eyes. His were dark and strangely alluring.

Unexpectedly reluctant to take his hands from the silken strands of her white-blond hair, Derek fought the protective urge that was prompting him to take her into his arms. In spite of her willowy height, she seemed small and delicate, helpless somehow, and he instinctively wanted to offer comfort. Yet a responsive surge of desire had him dropping his hands in alarm when he realized he wanted to give a lot more. "Good."

The electric charge that jumped between them as he once again released her, to stand in awkward silence, brought Kristiana an odd sense of relief, even if his nearness still had her pulse jumping. She was safe with this man. He wouldn't hurt her. Not when his touch and manner were like those of a healer.

"Are you a doctor?" she asked.

Captivated by the wonder that had come into her gaze, Derek shook his head and smiled. He'd never seen anyone with eyes like hers. Pale blue, a shade like no other he'd ever encountered. "No. Never quite made it." He reached up to touch the smudge on her cheek and was again aware of how close they were, of the delicate bone structure of her face and the feminine grace of her body. He gestured brusquely, disgusted with himself and his overactive libido. He was obviously more tired than he'd thought. "We better get going."

A bright smile curved her lips. "You will take me with you?"

"I'm not going to leave you out here in the middle of nowhere." He escorted her around the car to the passenger side and opened the door. "I've got to get you someplace where that arm can be looked at."

Kristiana sank into the lush seat of the vehicle with a grateful sigh. The man would help her get away from her ruined spacecraft, but she had to be wary of his kindness. It presented danger. She couldn't let him take her to a hospital. She wasn't from Earth, and if her body makeup and chemistry were basically the same, there were still differences. Her heart, for one, was on the right, not the left, side of her chest, and anyone making that discovery would bring attention she did not need or want.

"What may I call you?"

"My name's Derek Carpenter," he told her as he slid behind the steering wheel and turned to look at her. In the glow from the overhead light, her gaze was clear and direct. "You?"

"Kristiana."

Only a first name, not a last. He didn't question her further, but nodded acceptance. "Okay, Kristiana. Let's head for Chicago and get your arm taken care of."

He accelerated onto the highway, and she bit her lip. "My arm is fine. Really. It is only a scratch." He didn't answer, and she hurried on, admiring the cool, competent way he controlled his land vehicle even as she sought to change his mind about where they were going. "It does not hurt very much. I only need a . . ." What was the word? She floundered for a moment. "Bandage."

Frowning at the road, Derek bit back a denial. The torn flesh he'd seen was more than "a scratch," but a fear of hospitals wasn't uncommon. He had more than one friend who dreaded the smell of antiseptic and the sting of iodine. Yet, he suspected her desire to avoid an emergency room had little to do with anxiety over needles. He glanced at her and found her watching him too closely. She was either running away or didn't have any money to pay for the care. He decided to change the subject. For the moment.

In the darkness of the car, he'd become conscious of the quality of her speech. She had a gentle lilt to her words that he didn't recognize. "Where are you from, Kristiana?"

Searching for a good response, she chose the last place she had visited on the planet, a lovely, wide-open stretch of rugged land running beside towering mountains. "Wyoming."

"Really? You don't sound like any cowgirl I've ever met."

"There is something wrong with my words?" she asked in alarm. Normally, she was very good with languages.

"No, it's your accent. It's unusual." He shrugged off the impression. "Tell me, what brings you to Chicago? A job?"

Not the best of liars, Kristiana was glad for the black of night that kept her expression hidden. "Yes."

"And what do you do?"

She frowned, trying to think in Earth terms for a credible occupation, but somehow she didn't think he would believe she was an explorer. She decided on evasion. "Anything I have to."

Derek laughed, a rich sound that had her smiling and admiring the strength of his profile.

"And what of you? You said you are not a doctor?"

He shook his head. "No, but I'd once planned to be." Another quick glance showed him her puzzled frown, and he shrugged once more. "I went to medical school, but it wasn't for me."

"But you would make a good doctor."

"No, I wouldn't. Patients die no matter how hard a doctor tries to save them, and I couldn't deal with that frustration, the feeling of helplessness. So, instead of treating people directly, I help the physicians caring for them. I own a pharmaceutical company."

"You make medicine?"

"My company does. Carpenter Pharmaceuticals." At her silence he added, "We do a lot of research, too, trying to find answers to why people get cancer and other diseases and how to cure them. Success is hard to come by, but I think it's worth the fight."

She watched him in unspoken admiration. On her world, the practice of medicine was an honored occupation. Space travel was a necessity her people had mastered to survive, but healing and saving lives was something they were still struggling with even at its most rudimentary levels.

"We work with prosthetics, too. At least in that area we can see quick results."

"I know someone who lost a leg."

Derek smiled. "Then we probably helped him."

Kristiana shook her head. "I wish you could have." Without the proper technology, her friend had been condemned to using a clumsy wooden replica of a limb that often caused more pain than it relieved. She blinked back tears. "Your family must be very proud of you."

The flash of pain Derek felt at her words was quick but strong. He'd been close to his parents. There'd been only the three of them, no other relatives, his entire life. He'd felt their loss deeply. "I don't have a family."

"I am sorry."

He shoved aside the hurt that had dulled only a little with time. "Don't be. I'm used to being alone." He eased the car off the county highway and up a ramp onto the expressway that would eventually lead to the streets of Chicago.

"It must be difficult for you," Kristiana ventured.

Derek shrugged. "I grew up an only child. No sisters or brothers or aunts or uncles. And my parents were only children, too. When they died, I lost what family I had."

"You have no wife or children?"

"No, I never married." But there'd been women since his aborted engagement to Valerie in medical school. Ann, for one. With her, he had even come close to walking down the aisle. But ultimately it hadn't felt quite right.

A frown touched his mouth. He was beginning to think the family he'd always wanted was never going to happen. Abruptly shoving his gloomy thoughts aside, he turned back to Kristiana. "And you? Do you have family?"

Her smile was instantaneous. "My parents and a brother, Roham."

"Interesting name. Is he older or younger than you?"

"Older."

"And wiser?"

She laughed. "Yes, I think so."

Derek smiled as he guided the car along the expressway. Her laughter was free and light. It lifted his mood and eased the tension that always seemed to be coiled inside him, ready to drive him into action. "Does he know you're here?"

"Not yet."

"And what will he say when he finds out?"

"He will be worried," Kristiana said, and bit her lip as she thought of her brother. He was on another vessel returning to the mother ship. He would be upset when she wasn't there on his return, and he would be more so when her distress beacon arrived.

"It's nice to have someone to worry about you."

Kristiana pulled her thoughts back to the man named Derek Carpenter. "And who worries about you?"

He frowned. "My secretary?"

"Is she why you are hurrying back to Chicago at such a late hour?"

A bark of laughter filled the car as Derek tried to picture the stout but efficient, gray-haired Ms. Maggie Kirkpatrick waiting anxiously for him to arrive home. "No."

Kristiana frowned. "Then why do you hurry home so late?"

Derek shook his head. "I was just asking myself the same question." His eyes met hers in the light of the dash. He was intrigued by her even though he didn't want to be. "And what about you? Who are you rushing to meet? Or, should I ask, who are you running *from?*"

Chapter Two

His question caught her by surprise. The truth of her presence wasn't something she was prepared to explain. Alone, she had no one to go to, only those she needed to stay away from. But how could she convince him to accept her situation without arousing his suspicions? Managing to move her shoulders in what she hoped was a gesture of indifference, Kristiana shook her head. "No one is expecting me, and I do not think anyone will follow where I go."

Derek's frown returned. "There's no one waiting for you in Chicago? You're here on your own?" It wasn't that Kristiana didn't seem able to take care of herself. She was old enough, an adult, but somehow, she seemed vulnerable. "You have no place to stay when you get there?"

"I will find something," she hastily assured him.

"Do you have any money?"

"No, but..."

He swore under his breath. "You've hitchhiked to a strange city where you don't know anybody, you have no money, nowhere to stay and no job. *How* are you going to find something? How are you going to eat?"

"I have some things in my bag," she assured him, pulling what looked like a backpack from the rear floor of the car.

"And how long will that last?"

She shrank back against the seat and away from his angry glare. Somehow she didn't think any answer she gave would satisfy him.

Heavy silence filled the car, and Derek struggled with his temper. He had no right to be mad at or even concerned about the woman beside him. She meant nothing to him. He tried to shove some of his worry aside. "How's your arm?"

Kristiana self-consciously put a hand over the bruised skin. It was starting to throb. "Fine. It does not hurt."

He swore again, having no doubt that she wasn't telling the truth. "You don't have anyone to call, you won't go to the hospital, and I'll be damned if I'll dump you on a street corner."

"I would be—"

"Don't you dare say fine!"

Kristiana made herself as small as possible in her seat as more angry words cut the air.

"You're coming home with me."

"I . . ."

"I won't take no for an answer."

His dark eyes found hers, and she hastily nodded agreement.

"I'm not going to waste my time worrying about you. I'm going to know exactly where and how you are."

Suddenly his anger made sense to her. "You would worry for me?"

He caught her smile in the darkness. "Yes, and don't look so happy about it."

But knowing he cared about her, even a little, was enough to make her heart pound and cause a warm glow to touch her skin. "I was right. You would have made a good doctor."

"I..." The retort died when he looked at Kristiana again and found himself enveloped by eyes that shone with a wealth of trust, admiration and faith. No one had ever given such confidence to him so quickly, and he was astonished to feel the heat of embarrassment creeping up his neck. "I... Just sit back and relax. It won't be much longer."

She smiled and did as she was told—sat back and watched him drive. She'd never been in one of Earth's land vehicles before, but the big machine worked well. On her planet, standard transportation had evolved beyond wheels long ago, and space travel had become an everyday occurrence. It was in other scientific areas that her people lagged behind those on Earth. They were trying to catch up, but it was a slow and painful process.

Ahead in the distance, Chicago's muddled skyline glistened. Pinpoints of light twinkled across the horizon from various-sized buildings thrusting upward toward the stars.

Kristiana sat forward in her seat as she stared at the wonderful mixture of metal and wood and rock that made up an Earth city. Buildings on her world were almost exclusively of metal, all having a standard shape, if variations, in size. The diversity of the structures that those on Earth worked and lived in stirred her imagination.

"It is beautiful."

Derek looked anew at the view he had grown too accustomed to seeing and smiled. It *was* beautiful. He glanced across the seat at her. "Never been to Chicago before?"

She shook her head and, watching her, Derek's smile grew. With the city lights reflecting across the freeway, her awe was easy to see.

"You're not from a big city?" he asked, giving his attention to the road once more.

"I live in a small city."

He frowned, and remembered the slick jumpsuit she wore and the small backpack. A fancy new outfit and as little of the past as she wanted to bring to the future? His frown deepened. Was she running away from some unhappy yesterday to what she hoped was a bigger, brighter tomorrow? "I don't live in the city, either," he said. "I live in one of the suburbs."

And, as if in confirmation, the freeway curved away from the distant glow of the city toward the dimmer, less-traveled roads, where elegant houses were surrounded by manicured lawns. At nearly two in the morning, no windows were lit against the night, only porch lamps, but Kristiana was impressed when a garage door opened at the flick of a button and Derek drove into a building adjoining a two-story home that was easily twice the size of her own.

"You live here all alone?"

Derek cut the engine and grinned at her look of disbelief. "This was my parents' home." He'd returned to it and to what had been rather than remaining in what was, at the time, a large apartment and a relationship that was coming apart. He had thought he and Ann would marry eventually. Planned on and hoped for it. But the varying interests that had brought and kept them together had, after too many months of sometimes uncomfortable compromise, forced them both to realize that, no matter how much they wanted it to work, they didn't belong together. "I moved back in when they died."

Kristiana recognized the lingering pain of loss and failure he thought was hidden. "You miss them."

"Sometimes very much." It was an admission that surprised him, and, facing her in the darkness of the garage as overhead the door groaned to a close behind them, his unwilling fascination with her grew.

Kristiana was a mystery. In the course of a few hours she'd made him mad, sad and even happy, but a small-town girl come to try her luck in the big city? He didn't think so. Intelligence lay behind her gaze, as did experience. She'd seen more of life than what a close-knit, country community could offer. Yet she carried an air of naiveté, too. It was an odd but appealing combination. His finger lifted to brush the softness of her cheek. "We need to look at that arm."

When he turned away to slide out of the car, it was as if someone had cut the rope that was holding her up. Without him next to her, she felt suddenly alone and lost, and she hastened to follow, at least, she tried to. Confronted with myriad buttons and levers on the door panel next to her, she wasn't sure which one to use to get out of the vehicle. Afraid of being left behind, she pushed one and pressed another, but nothing happened.

"What are you doing?"

She turned to find him leaning down to look at her through the open driver's side door. "Trying to get out."

A grin spread across his mouth, and he pointed. "The silver lever."

She pulled, metal snapped, and the door swung open. She tumbled out but wasn't given a chance to look around. Catching her good arm, Derek led her out of the garage and into his house, not slowing down until he reached the upstairs bathroom.

"Sit."

She followed his gesture to the long counter surrounding the sink and slipped up onto it, but she didn't watch him as he pushed aside a mirror that hid a box in the wall. Instead she gazed around at the plush towels, the shining blue and beige ceramic tiles and a huge porcelain tub. A more luxurious sanitation station she could not remember seeing, but it and all it held was quickly forgotten when he touched her arm.

Feeling her jerk in his grasp, Derek stilled as startled pain filled her eyes. "Doesn't hurt, huh?"

Ashamed for her earlier untruth, she lowered her gaze from his to the scissors in his hand. "Only a little."

"You're not a very good liar."

"That is what Roham says."

"He's right." Derek stopped talking and gave his full attention to her arm. Cutting away some material from her sleeve, he exposed the gash in her flesh from end to end. His face was grim as he reached for a bottle of antiseptic. "This is going to sting."

She gasped as the cotton ball he was using touched her skin, but stayed still as the liquid on it bubbled and hissed across the wound.

"You could probably use a couple of stitches." Scowling at her from under his eyebrows, he dampened a new cotton ball to clean the cut again.

"Stitches?" She didn't relish the idea of her flesh being sewn.

"We'll make do with some butterfly strips."

She started to question his using an insect on her wound, but any doubts as to his intent died as she watched him work. His touch was strong and sure, his fingers able in their task. Her arm was burning sharply from the attention it was receiving, but it was obvious Derek knew what he was doing. Shoving away the pain, she concentrated on him rather than on his ministrations to her arm.

His blond hair was darker than that of those on her world, and he appeared taller and broader, especially in the confines of the small room. Curling her hand into a fist in her lap, she had to resist the urge to reach out to wipe the wrinkles from his brow as he frowned. And she felt again, the magnetic pull that had shot between them as they'd stood on the highway in the dark. It was a shock to realize she was attracted to him, a man of Earth. She'd never felt such empathy for an alien before.

He glanced up, and she looked away, but not quickly enough. The warmth she was feeling had evidently spread to him with a rush; his jaw clenched. Suddenly Derek found it difficult to ignore the soft heat of her skin as he held her arm. He struggled to put his reaction and the cotton ball calmly aside. "This looks as if it's more than a cut. Were you burned?"

Kristiana remembered the flames in her control panel, the black smoke, the blaring alarm and the cold fear of being trapped, and nodded sharply.

He shook his head. "How did you do this? Did you build a fire to try to stay warm?" Spring nights in Illinois could be chilly.

"Yes," she agreed, quick to grab any explanation he gave. But she missed the suspicion that came into his gaze by watching his fingers instead of his face. "I fell."

He didn't believe her, but that was beside the point. He turned from her to cross the room to a potted plant. With long green spines, it sat on a shelf where the sun would hit it during the day.

When he broke off one of its branches and carried it back to squeeze some of its liquid on her wound, Kristiana put out a hand to touch the weeping leaf.

"This is medicine?"

"Aloe. You've never seen it before?"

She shook her head and watched as he applied the liquid from the leaf to the skin around the wound. The soothing sensation was instant.

"I believe that for every illness on earth, there's a natural cure—like this—to help us heal," he told her.

"Do you think that's true on every planet?" As soon as the words were out, Kristiana regretted them, but it was too late. She held her breath and watched him smile as he continued to work on her arm.

"That's a strange question." He shrugged. "But I don't see why not." He put the aloe aside and reached for some ointment. "We waste a lot of time on earth creating synthetic medicine. If we devoted more energy to working with Mother Nature instead of against her, I think we'd get further ahead."

"What do you mean?"

"I mean, we should be saving and studying the rain forest and the old-growth trees in the northwest. Many of our medicines come from the rain forest, and scientists recently found a possible lead for a cancer cure in the bark of those old-growth trees by the Pacific. Instead of cutting them down, we ought to be protecting them and other natural resources."

She watched him pick up the scissors again.

"Take dandelions, for instance. We spend our time trying to kill them off, but the Indians used them for medicine, and so did other cultures. Dandelion tea was prescribed as a natural diuretic." He sighed. "But modern science hasn't proven our friendly weed's worth yet, so it remains an enemy in our grass instead of an ally on our pharmacy shelves." He looked up at her. "You're going to lose the sleeve of this suit."

"I have another."

He grunted, and she watched him with growing wonder. The efforts of her planet's medical people to find cures were bumbling at best. They didn't know where to look or how to go about it. But this man would. He would know how to find the medicine her people needed. But she couldn't ask for his help. Not for more than her own meager needs.

She bit her lip and fought the need to ask more.

"You've had your tetanus shot?" Derek asked as he cut the sleeve off and threw it along with the used cotton balls into a wastebasket on the floor.

"I do not think so," she answered with a frown that earned a glare.

"You'll get one on Monday when we go to work."

"Work?"

"You need a job. You're obviously interested in medicine. Why not come work for me?"

Kristiana opened her mouth to protest. Her people's previous visits to earth had been confined to small towns and out-of-the-way places. It made coming and going easier—and it would make her rescue safer. To retrieve her from a place as big as his Chicago would be difficult, much more tricky. But the possibility of learning more about medicine..."I will come."

"Not even going to ask what I pay?" he asked with a grin as he grabbed a roll of gauze and began to wind it around her arm.

"Whatever it is, it will be enough."

He shook his head. "Wait until you see what they charge for rent around here. You may change your mind, but maybe we can find someone for you to bunk with." Yet even as he made the suggestion, Derek found himself disliking the possibility. He didn't want her to be with anyone else.

Kristiana jumped when his fingers abruptly ripped the gauze with a brutal jerk, and she looked to his face in surprise. He was scowling. "You are angry at me? You do not have to give me a job."

He sighed and began piling the medical supplies back in the medicine cabinet. "No, I'm not angry. I'm tired. And I'm not *giving* you a job. You're going to work for it." He snapped the cabinet door shut, and his eyes locked with hers. The pull was there instantly, the need to touch, the want to hold. He fought it. "Come on. I'll show you where to sleep."

Following in his wake, Kristiana was finding it difficult to breathe—again. Whenever Derek Carpenter looked at her, her heart seemed to stop beating. He paused in a doorway, swept her past him with a gesture. She hurried to comply lest the heat of his body burn hers as she brushed by.

"Look through the drawers for a nightgown. My mother always kept extra clothes for guests. I never bothered to clean the drawers." He frowned. Because he'd never had any guests. He'd remained by himself in the house. Until now.

Abruptly he turned to go, but she stopped him. "How long have they been gone?"

His brows drew together in question.

"Your mother and father."

"Two years." Two centuries. He suddenly felt as if he'd been alone forever. His eyes sought hers once more and clung. First his drive, his need to find the elusive purpose to his life, had separated him from others, then his grief had further isolated him. But just by being with him tonight, somehow Kristiana had freed him from his painful solitude. With her, he wasn't by himself anymore—and he no longer wanted to be. "Get some sleep."

The gravelly demand nearly buckled her knees as the door closed behind him, and she reached out to grab hold of the dresser to keep from sinking to the floor. Never had a man had such an effect on her as Derek Carpenter did. He was strong, attractive in a way she had never expected, and gentle with the touch of a healer. He captivated and terrified. On a strange planet, he was savior and friend. With their separate worlds and their different ways, it wasn't possible that he could be more.

WAKING HOURS LATER to the warm glow of the sun and the hum of voices, Kristiana quickly shrugged into the knee-length, pink robe that matched the nightgown she'd found in the dresser. She followed the light and the sound of conversation down the carpeted stairs to a large room lined with long windows and filled with bulky but homey furniture. A big-screen monitor was flashing pictures and announcing the news of the planet.

Stopping in front of what she knew earthlings called a television set, Kristiana studied the equipment and compared it to those she'd seen in an appliance store on

her last visit. The Earth version of television was behind her planet's in technology, but Earthlings were
rapidly approaching more sophisticated modes of
communication.

"You're up."

She jumped at the greeting and spun around to find
Derek leaning against the doorway, watching her. Gone
was the formal attire of suit and tie he'd worn the night
before. Instead he was dressed in a simple T-shirt and
jeans, leaning against the doorway. The way the material clung to the hard lines of his body had her throat
drying up. She managed to avoid the magnetic pull of
his gaze to focus on the cup in his hand.

"Coffee?" he asked, following her gaze, and shoving his free hand into his jeans' pocket to stop from
reaching out to touch her as she moved toward him. Her
sleep-tousled hair and the soft, flowing robe magnified
the air of vulnerability he'd sensed in her the night before, and in the light of day he found she was even
lovelier than he'd remembered. "You must be hungry."

She put a hand over her stomach. "Very."

He grinned and turned to lead her into the kitchen,
but she stopped at the door.

The room was a wonder of gleaming machinery. She
recognized some of it but didn't know how to use most.
Computers had taken away much of the necessity to
cook or otherwise prepare meals on her world. To eat,
it was only necessary to make a request.

"What would you like? Eggs? Toast?" Kristiana
didn't answer immediately, and Derek frowned as he
watched her look around. The way she was staring, it
was if she'd never been in a kitchen before.

"Whatever you had would be fine," she told him, hastily putting her hands into her pockets. She was afraid to touch anything, and she knew next to nothing about Earth food. Once she'd convinced Roham to let her try something called ice cream that a man on a street corner had been selling, and it had been wonderful.

"Eggs and toast, then." He gestured to the stove. "There's the frying pan. Eggs and butter are in the fridge, along with milk and orange juice if you want them, and the toaster and bread are over here."

She watched him pat the counter upon which sat a sleek white piece of plastic and a gaily wrapped loaf.

"I'll be in watching the news."

She managed to return his smile as he left the room, but she was sorely tempted to call him back. Yet, to admit she didn't know how to use the standard kitchen appliances would be to admit she wasn't from Earth. Smothering a sigh, she walked to the big metal refrigerator and pulled open the top door. A cloud of freezing air hit her face and she immediately snapped it shut in favor of the bigger door beneath it. She quickly spotted the eggs. Those, at least, she recognized.

Eggs were common to most worlds, though they took different shapes, sizes and colors. She stopped in front of the microwave oven set on a countertop and wondered if it worked as well as her replicator. With a sigh, and deciding it was better to follow Derek's advice, she put the eggs into the pan.

Discarding the shells, she found herself faced with an array of buttons on and around the stove. She tried one, and took four tries before she managed to activate the gas under the pan. Relieved that the high blue flame finally had the eggs sizzling, she crossed the room to the bread and what Derek had called the toaster.

Frowning at the plastic-and-metal contraption, she put two slices of bread into its slots and waited, but nothing happened. Bending to examine the levers, she tried pushing the largest one, and the bread disappeared inside. She grinned, and her stomach growled in anticipation. But as the wires glowed hot around the slices, she wondered how she'd be able to tell when the bread was done and how she'd get it back out again.

Hearing the fan go on, Derek returned to the kitchen in time to see Kristiana bend over the toaster just as the bread popped out. The slices hit her in the face. Caught between laughter and disbelief, he forgot both as the smell of something burning erupted through the room. He spotted the high flames under the frying eggs and ran.

Clutching the toasted bread, Kristiana spun to watch him rescue the pan from the fire, but she wasn't prepared for the look of incredulity he leveled on her. She stammered. "I—I burned them?"

"You have given a whole new meaning to fried eggs," he responded dryly, and flicked off the gas. "You do know how to cook, don't you?"

"I..." His golden gaze narrowed on her. "No."

He sighed and found himself back at square one. Since rising, he'd been trying to find a logical reason behind Kristiana's appearance. Unwilling to accept her as a small-town girl escaping the confines of the farm for big-city life, he'd tossed out that possibility along with the chances of her being an abused runaway. She was evasive, even vulnerable, but she wasn't afraid. Not of touch, at least. She'd readily endured his cursory examination and had sat willingly through his ministrations. And she hadn't resisted or reacted adversely to the chemistry surging between them that had nearly robbed him of any sleep.

The only other possibility he'd been able to come up with was that perhaps she was Amish or from some other similar reclusive society or culture. That could account for her black wardrobe, the lack of contacts outside her "small city," and even the formal, lilting speech that could belie a Western accent. But he doubted any self-respecting Amish woman would be unable to fry an egg.

He shook his head. "I've heard of people who can't boil water, but I guess I never took the claim seriously. Sit down."

Subdued but grateful for his intervention, she slid onto one of the high stools positioned around an island in the center of the room.

"Here's some butter for your toast," he said, plopping a container and a knife in front of her. "Want some jam? All I have is strawberry."

"That is fine." While he busied himself at the stove, she figured out how to use the knife to spread first butter, then jam across the toast before taking a bite. The explosion of taste was wonderful, and she almost sighed out loud after the first swallow. Earth toast was not quite like anything she had previously tasted. She stared at the slice in her hand in speculation and concluded that the flavor had to come from the jam.

"Coffee?"

She looked up to find him standing in front of her with a cup and pot, and hastily put the bread aside. "Thank you."

"Cream or sugar?"

"Please."

He frowned as she pulled the cup he filled toward her and deeply inhaled its rich aroma. "Funny, you didn't strike me as the kind that needed the smell of coffee to wake up."

"Coffee wakes you up?"

"Some would say so," he said, pushing a bowl of sugar toward her.

"I . . . I just like the smell," she assured him at his puzzled look. Taking a heaping teaspoon of white crystals from the bowl he offered, she dropped the substance into her cup.

Her attempt to prove she knew what she was doing had him grinning. "Like a little coffee with your sugar?"

Trying to ignore his intent study of her movements and about to take a sip, she saw his amusement and wondered if she had done something wrong.

"Never mind. My father always did the same thing. Used to drive my mother nuts." But his father hadn't eaten everything as if he were tasting it for the first time.

Kristiana watched Derek return to the stove and the sizzling eggs, and chanced a sip of the dark brew. It was hot and sharp, but she thought she liked it. She tried another sip as Derek returned with a plateful of eggs and a fork. "Thank you."

"You're welcome."

His smile was disarming, and she felt her pulse flutter. "I am sorry to be so much bother."

"No bother."

Warm heat was creeping up her neck under his steady stare, and it was getting hard to breathe again. "I am not keeping you from your news?"

"You're much more interesting to watch."

Chapter Three

Kristiana nearly dropped her fork.

"But if I make you nervous, I'll go."

The eyes holding hers were warm with amusement — and something much deeper. But with a smile, he was gone and she was left to deal with a pounding heart and a pile of food the precise likes of which she had never seen or eaten before.

Yet it didn't take her long to finish. Like a moth drawn to a flame, she was eager to be with Derek. She left the kitchen to find him sprawled comfortably in a chair in front of the television.

He didn't look up when she entered the room, but he felt her presence. Too strongly. "Have enough to eat?"

"Yes, thank you." Uncertain of what to do, she knelt beside his chair and looked to the television monitor he seemed so intent on. "The news is good?"

"The news is the same as always. Some good, some bad." Out of the corner of his eye, he saw her reach for a book he'd left open on the coffee table.

"You are reading about your medicines?" she asked, studying the pictures and captions and seeking similarities between the plants she saw on paper and those back at her home.

"Yes, that's a book about Native American plant use."

"May I read it?"

"Of course." He watched her flip a page and immediately smile.

"Dandelions. You said you have some."

"To the horror of my neighbors, I have many—at least in the backyard."

She frowned. "They are afraid of your dandelions?"

He grinned. "Only to the extent that their yards keep collecting my seeds."

Not certain she understood, she nodded, nevertheless, as if she did. "I would like to see them."

"My neighbors?"

"Your dandelions."

His grin broadened. "Just look out the back window. But I'm afraid they're exactly the same as every other one you've seen before."

"Of course," she agreed gravely, but, looking down, she didn't see him frown at her serious response. "I will go upstairs and change so I can go outside."

She rose, and he followed the motion with a considering gaze. The way she talked, he was sometimes tempted to believe she was from another planet. "You'd better save your other jumpsuit for tomorrow. There're some clothes that might fit you in—"

"Just south of Chicago last night," the news announcer was saying, "several witnesses reported seeing a blinding streak of light crossing the sky around midnight."

Kristiana followed Derek's gaze to the television as her scarred and blackened spacecraft suddenly appeared on the screen.

"Authorities have announced that one of their old satellites has crashed to earth. They had expected it to burn up in the atmosphere upon reentry, but..."

Kristiana shook her head and missed the rest of the announcer's words as she focused on the pictures. What she'd feared had come true: her ship's self-destruct program hadn't worked correctly. It may have started, but the sequence hadn't finished. The door was open! Someone had gotten inside!

"That's what I must've seen last night," Derek told her, not taking his eyes from the screen. "Did you see it, too?"

She didn't hear him. Her attention was on the burned-out ship. Maybe all wasn't lost. Earth authorities may have gotten inside, but from the blackened ruins, it didn't appear that they would have found much.

"Kristiana?"

Startled back to the present, she pulled her gaze from the screen to find Derek sitting up straight in his chair, watching her.

"Are you all right?"

"Yes, I..."

"Are you dizzy? Is it your arm?"

He was on his feet instantly, but she adamantly shook her head at his approach. "I am fine. Really. It was just the television. It looks very bad."

Staring at her until he was satisfied she wasn't trying to cover up any illness, he finally nodded. "The satellite? Yes, they're lucky it crashed outside the city. No one on the ground was hurt."

"Authorities have secured the area since these pictures were taken earlier and request that people stay away from the site until they are certain all debris has been collected for analysis," the newscaster continued as the camera followed two men approaching the craft in the pale light of dawn. One was middle-aged and dark in coloring, the other young, tall and red-haired.

Kristiana started when, without warning, the picture flashed back to the female news announcer.

"The crash is not without its lighter side, of course," the woman remarked. "Locals are already speculating that this was not a satellite but a spaceship that crash-landed. Rumors are quickly circulating of an alien invader walking among us." Her smile as she glanced down to turn over another page of notes did not lend any credence to the possibility. "In California today..."

"I will go change," Kristiana abruptly announced and, before Derek could comment, she was out the door.

Startled by her hasty exit, he frowned after her before slowly allowing his gaze to return to the television. It was strange that a story about a satellite would bother her, but maybe she'd seen it the night before and it had frightened her. Or...

Derek shook his head and sank back in the chair. He wasn't having a close encounter, but he was having an encounter—one of the most interesting kind... His frown deepened. He had a lot of questions about and for Kristiana, and he was determined to get an answer to every one.

Out of sight and behind the closed bedroom door, Kristiana's fingers trembled as she shuffled through the dresser drawers for something to wear. The fear of discovery was strong, but reason told her that she was safe. Far from the crash site, no one would find her even if they did, somehow, conclude that someone had managed to escape the craft. They would have no way to follow her. She wouldn't be caught.

Pulling a navy blue T-shirt like the one Derek wore from the drawer, she stopped to stare at herself in the mirror. But she scarcely even saw her image.

With most of the worlds her people visited, capture was not something to guard against. Traders of goods and knowledge, she and her companions were welcomed in a universe of space commerce. But Earth was not part of that network. It was one of the few places her people came unannounced—and afraid.

As observers, studiers of a world and a society that was so much like their own but that had evolved differently, they feared being caught and caged above any other hazard during an Earth mission.

For, out of space but fascinated by it, Earthlings treated outworlders as specimens in a lab, aliens to be studied, rather than welcomed as envoys. Being dissected alive, with no chance for freedom, she or any of her people could live out the rest of their lives alone, aware and in agony within a confinement they would never be able to escape.

Whirling from the dresser, Kristiana abruptly went to her backpack and reassured herself that the homing beacon was still blinking. Her people would come. Her people would find her. She would not be deserted. She would be saved. But until that happened, she was safe. Derek would not allow her to be harmed. Finding strength in thinking of him, her gaze moved to one of the windows and, following the sun on its panes, she looked out at a green lawn covered with yellow flowers. She recognized them instantly. "Dandelions."

Throwing off the night wear and jumping into the T-shirt and a pair of pants that were a bit too short and baggy, she left the room and romped barefoot down the stairs and straight out the back door.

Derek heard the screen door slam and rose to follow the sound. When he got to the doorway, his grin came without thought. Kristiana was down on her hands and knees, smelling the dandelions. He opened the door to join her, but before he could step outside, a flash of brown and an angry growl ripped past the porch.

Derek froze. His neighbor's dog. Big and mean and constantly breaking loose to roam the yards—especially Derek's, because the latch on the iron gate was broken—the German shepherd wasn't an animal to mess with. And Kristiana was right in its path.

"Kristiana! Watch out!" Even as he shouted, Derek began to run. Blindly racing across the porch, he grabbed a shovel from where it rested against the railing and hurtled down the steps. But as he heaved the heavy tool to his shoulder, his steps faltered.

Ahead of him Kristiana was still on her knees in the grass, but she wasn't cowering in fear at the shepherd. She was smiling and holding out her hand to the dog, whose toothy sneer had miraculously turned into a slurping smile and whose snarl had become a plaintive whine.

The shovel drooped in Derek's grip, and he cautiously made his way forward as the huge German shepherd fell to the ground to roll belly-up for a tummy rub. "I don't believe it."

Kristiana turned to smile up at him. "He is yours?"

"My neighbor's, and that animal is the most vicious thing for blocks around."

She frowned. "He is only defending what he sees as his territory." She laughed as the dog jumped up on all fours again.

Disbelieving but willing to let bygones be bygones, Derek reached out to pet the shepherd, too, but was met with a decisive snap of sharp teeth. He pulled his hand back. "See!"

Kristiana scowled at the dog and then at him. "It is your own fault."

"Mine?" Derek asked in amazement.

"You always yell at him."

"I..." He cleared his throat when her eyebrow quirked. "I do." And he loved animals. Except for this one.

"Would you be friendly to someone who yells at you all the time?"

Derek shrugged. "I suppose not." He sighed as he watched her scratch the dog's head. "I don't suppose you can convince him to leave. I've never been able to get him out of the yard without his owner's help."

"You want him to go?" She smiled at the dog, kissed its head, and waved. In a flash the shepherd was gone, and Derek was left staring after the animal in bemusement.

"How'd you do that?"

"No one likes to stay where he or she is not wanted."

"You told him..." Derek stared at the gate that hung drunkenly on its hinges across the yard.

"You do not believe people can talk to animals?" she questioned, forgetting for the moment that communication with another species was something Earth humans had not yet mastered.

"I've never been very good at it," he told her as she brushed her long hair over her shoulder. His attention returned to the gate as he searched for a logical explanation for the easy rapport she'd had with the dog. Hand signals perhaps?

"But you believe it is possible?"

Only half listening and still trying to figure out how she'd controlled the animal, he turned to meet the sincere blue of her direct gaze and shrugged. "I suppose."

She frowned. "Surely you have heard of people who can move objects with their mind?" It was a skill she was still perfecting, but it was the same principle she wanted him to understand.

"Of course."

"Why can they do it and you not?"

He moved his shoulders again. "I don't know."

"Perhaps they use parts of their brain you have yet to develop." At his frown, she added, "It has been proven that humans do not use at least eighty percent of their brain."

"And science hasn't figured out why."

She smiled. "See? You can talk to animals. You simply have not yet learned how."

He grinned. Obviously, if she had a secret way of making animals perform on command, she wasn't going to let him in on it. He sagged to his knees in the grass beside her, ready to play along. "And you have?"

She wrinkled her nose. "Sometimes." His eyes, as they lingered on her, were very steady, and a self-conscious heat began creeping into her cheeks. "You are looking at me very oddly."

"I'm just trying to figure you out."

"I am that strange?"

"That unique." To resist the sudden urge to touch her, he leaned back in the grass on one elbow and stretched his legs out in front of him. "Maybe that newscast was right. Maybe it wasn't a satellite that crashed to earth. Maybe it was a spaceship, and you're the alien who escaped.''

Petrified, Kristiana stared at him, suddenly unable to speak or move. He'd found her out!

Derek grinned at her stricken expression. Having spoken his insane idea out loud, it sounded ludicrous. ''You're from Venus, right? Or is it Mars?''

It was a heart-stopping moment before she realized he was laughing at her, and Kristiana breathed again and hurried to follow his lead. ''Venus is too hot, and Mars is too dry.''

''Pluto, then.''

''Too cold.''

His grin grew at the haughty tilt of her chin. ''Well, Wyoming *is* practically another planet . . .''

Her mouth fell open. ''It is not!''

''Where are you from in Wyoming? What small city?''

Her gaze dropped from his as she searched for a name she couldn't remember. ''Why do you want to know?''

''Because I want to know more about you.''

Her eyes flew back to his, and the warmth in his golden gaze had her blood suddenly pumping hotly. She fumbled for something to say and caught at a dandelion nestled in the grass between them. ''May I pick one?''

His indifferent gesture toward the dandelion belied the emotions making his fingers curl tightly over a helpless piece of grass. ''Pick as many as you like.''

''Really?''

Her brilliant smile had his stomach somersaulting, and his original question was abruptly forgotten. ''Really.'' And she did. He sat and watched as she roamed the yard, gathering as many of the yellow weeds as she could carry before rejoining him with her booty. He plucked one of the sticky stems from her fingers. "I used to bring my mother bouquets of dandelions all the time."

Kristiana smiled. "She liked them?"

"She liked the thought." He pointed to the flowers. "What are you going to do with these?"

"I wanted to see if I could make dandelion tea."

"Do you have an upset stomach?"

His questioning smile made her feel silly and shy all at once. "No, I was simply wondering how. Your book says some medicinal brews are made from the roots of plants, others from the leaves, and still more from the flowers. Which do you think it is for the dandelions? And how can you tell the difference?"

Her face was serious as she studied the flowers. Derek couldn't doubt that she really wanted to know, and, strangely moved, he reached out to catch her chin with his fingers.

"Let's go read the book and find out."

BUT THE BOOK hadn't been nearly detailed enough— not when her enthusiasm was so infectious and not when it involved a subject he was so interested in. It hadn't been long before they were in the car and touring the gardens, exotic and ordinary, throughout the area, and poring over books on herbal medicine as they visited each and every center.

As they traveled from place to place, it occurred to Kristiana that she should be afraid. She was alone on a strange world, surrounded by a people she did not know. Except for one. But that only made it impossible to feel fear, especially when his fingers found and held hers in a simple gesture of care and possession.

Derek didn't know how her hand gotten into his. Had she put it there, or had he taken it? Whichever the case, he enjoyed the sensation as well as the sharing. By the time the sun was setting, he had ceased to wonder.

"Are you hungry?" he asked as they exited yet another greenhouse.

Kristiana looked back at the sunlit glass structure where she had seen an extensive herb garden and had enjoyed the warmth of Derek's guiding touch as he'd explained the properties of various plants. He was touching her still. His palm rested against hers and their fingers were entwined.

"Yes."

"How about a hamburger?"

His smile warmed her clear down to the toes. "If you have one, too."

He laughed and pulled her toward the car.

Derek hadn't realized until they were nearly home, with Kristiana still munching on some french fries from a takeout, that he hadn't thought of the office all day—and that was after being out of it for nearly a week in Indianapolis. He couldn't remember a time when he hadn't been consumed by work or studies or some special project.

"You are quiet," Kristiana observed.

He glanced over at her as the house came into view. "I was thinking. Couldn't you smell the smoke?"

"The smoke?" she asked with a frown.

He laughed and turned into the driveway, activating the garage door opener. "That's supposed to be a joke."

"A joke?"

"Yes. You know, funny, ha, ha." He pulled the car to a halt in the garage and turned to her.

"Oh," she said, and managed a baffled smile.

"You *are* from planet Mars."

"I am not!" But he was already getting out of the car. She grabbed the silver lever and followed him out of the vehicle and into the house.

"When we go into work tomorrow," he told her over his shoulder, "I'm going to have to call you something besides Kristiana. What's your last name?"

Watching him as he stopped at the coffee table to toss his keys onto a shelf by the television, she fumbled for an answer. He would never be able to pronounce her family name. She had to find an Earth substitute and one jumped out at her from the book on plants lying in front of her. "Cooke."

Turning as she looked up, he shoved his hands into his pockets. "With an *e?*"

"Yes."

Fidgeting, she walked away from the table and the source of her lie.

Derek's eyes fell to the book he knew so well, the author's name emblazoned boldly across the cover.

"What a coincidence."

The murmur was so soft Kristiana didn't hear it as she moved toward the staircase. "I think I will go upstairs."

"I think we both should."

Her eyes widened on his in surprise.

"I need to look at that arm," he explained.

Trapped by his golden gaze, she froze where she stood and watched him cross the room with long, steady strides to join her by the steps. His hand settled on her waist as they started to climb, and her heart began to pound. His touch was hot, and when they reached the bathroom and his fingers ran up her arm, she felt as if she'd been scorched.

Not unaware of the tension beginning to boil between them, Derek kept his hands busy with the medical supplies to stop them from pulling her close. "It might sting a little when I pull the gauze off."

She licked dry lips—and regretted the motion immediately when his eyes fastened on her mouth.

"Hold still," he said, his jaw clenching as he put the scissors to the thin, white cotton around her arm. The angry cut underneath was enough to distract his attention from baser emotions. "You definitely need to get a tetanus shot tomorrow."

"It is bad?" Her heart jumped in fear. People on her planet could die from infections caused by little scratches, much less big ones such as hers.

"It's clean, and I don't think it's festering." He scowled at the raw flesh. "But it's going to hurt for quite a while before it heals."

"But I will get better?"

"I don't see why not." He stepped away for more aloe, followed by antibiotic ointment. "I'll give you some aspirin tonight. I should have given you some yesterday."

"Aspirin?"

"It'll help the pain and inflammation." His fingers gently worked the gash on her arm. "Aspirin's not just for headaches."

Her eyes lifted to his.

"Did you sleep last night?"

The innocent question had her heart jumping into her throat, and her startled, wide blue eyes reflected what she was feeling all too clearly.

Derek's jaw worked again, and he fought to keep his attention focused on needs other than desire. "Your arm didn't bother you?" he managed to clarify.

She shook her head, unable to find her voice. He was still watching her, and she was unable to look away.

"Good."

His concentration returned to her arm, and she let out the breath she'd unknowingly held.

"You'd better lock your door tonight."

The sudden pronouncement made her frown. "Why?"

"So nothing else bothers you."

The burning gold-brown of his gaze on her warned exactly of what the "nothing" was, and she swallowed tightly. Without watching what he was doing, he began to rebind her arm with gauze. Only when he was done did his eyes leave hers.

"Are you afraid of me, Kristiana?"

"No." The word was no more than a whisper. His hip rested against her thigh as she sat on the counter. His body was hot. As hot as hers.

"You should be."

Time stopped when, only inches apart, she once more found herself captured by a gaze darker than her own. His breath mingled with hers. Hesitantly, almost imperceptibly, she leaned forward. And he moved away.

"You'd better call it a night," he said, abruptly turning to put the supplies back into the medicine cabinet. "We'll need to be up early to drive to work, and it's been a busy day."

She slipped off the counter and moved toward the door.

"Your aspirin."

Stopping, she turned back to him and watched as he shook two round pills from a white bottle. When he held them out to her, she reached to take them and the tips of his fingers brushed her palm. The sparks his touch set off raced up her arm, and the jolt had her hand trembling as she accepted the glass of water that followed. Somehow she swallowed both pills. "Thank you."

A cool eyebrow arched over a brooding eye. "Don't forget to lock the door."

Chapter Four

The trip to Derek's office in the morning was an experience to remember. Cars were rushing everywhere in lane after lane of traffic. Kristiana found it a wonder anyone arrived anywhere in one piece because the Chicago freeway at rush hour was worse than any space dock she had ever seen. But at least the haphazardly moving vehicles kept her attention off the man beside her.

Derek had all but ignored her since rebandaging her arm the night before. It wasn't a hostile silence separating them, but it was uncomfortable nonetheless. She was too aware of him and he too aware of her. But he hadn't tried to bother her when she was sleeping. She knew because she'd lain awake waiting for the handle on the door to turn.

Smothering a sigh, she glanced at him as he drove competently through the rapidly dodging cars. Her attraction to him was unexpected but not unusual. Beings from different worlds often mated, but she could recall no such union that involved a man or woman from Earth. It was an unspoken taboo; Earthlings were to be left alone until such time as the planet was ready to join the legion of outworlders who used space as their highway.

Yet even if she was willing to throw caution and good sense to the wind, Derek didn't seem prepared to consummate any relationship with her. He was fighting the invisible force vibrating between them.

Kristiana frowned. She knew his resistance should make her grateful. Becoming involved with him would only make it harder to leave when rescue arrived. Still, the possibility already had her almost regretting the need to go.

"I hope you're not disappointed at not working downtown," Derek said, turning his head briefly to find her watching him. "Being out in the western suburbs has proven a better location for us."

"I do not mind." She looked warily out at the cars still buzzing around them. "Perhaps the streets will be less busy there."

His grin was like quicksilver, fast and brilliant, cutting through the wary quiet that had been keeping them apart.

Trying to resist his feelings for her was futile, Derek realized. The chemistry was there. It was useless to fight feelings, but he did have to find a way to deal with them. She was under his protection while under his roof. Out of her depth in a city she knew nothing about, she was alone except for him. It put him at a disadvantage, and he didn't like it. He wasn't a patient man when it came to pursuing something he wanted. "You don't like our rush hour?"

"Everybody is certainly rushing," she agreed. "Does it really only last an hour?"

His grunted. "We should be so lucky."

Turning to him again, she found he wasn't looking at her anymore, but he was smiling. The tension was gone. Her mouth curved, too. He was no longer trying to hold her away from him but would let her close. Her heart skipped a beat. *How close* had yet to be determined.

A short time later, just outside Chicago's city limits, a tight conglomerate of three-story buildings came into sight. Sprawled across rolling land, the Carpenter Pharmaceutical complex appeared to be a metropolis unto itself.

The acreage was carefully landscaped with trees and bushes and flowers just beginning to burst with spring. The buildings, erect in white lines and dark windows, were bordered by a network of parking lots that led to various entrances. Beyond the largest lot sat a small helicopter pad ready to accommodate executive get-aways or rush-order supplies fresh from the field.

Following Derek from a parking space labeled with his name, Kristiana strained to take in everything. But her attention was drawn more to the man than the buildings he owned. She watched as the transformation from everyday citizen to a person of authority deepened with each step he took. The closer he came to his place of business, the larger and more imposing he seemed to become. His ability to command, to lead, to make decisions showed. He knew where he was going and could take others with him. Seeing him so reminded her of their first meeting. She had been intimidated by him, by his obvious strength and power, but now she also knew the gentleness behind the imposing executive demeanor.

"You are different here," she told him.

He glanced down at her, slowing his longer pace to match hers. "Different?"

"The way you project yourself. I think people listen to you here."

He laughed. "They'd better. I own the company."

"Derek!"

He stopped and turned, slipping his briefcase from his right to his left hand at another man's approach. "David."

The man named David put his hand into Derek's when he reached him, and Kristiana watched him smile. David was not as tall as Derek. He was dark where Derek was light, yet a similar sense of command clung to him. The shine of affection in his deep brown eyes said he was fond of Derek Carpenter. She immediately decided she liked this David.

"How'd it go in Indiana?" David asked, falling into step beside them.

Derek shrugged. "We should get a call today."

"Great!" David's smile reached out to Kristiana. "And who have we here?"

"Kristiana Cooke," Derek told him. "She's coming to work for us. Kristiana, this is David Mallory, my right hand."

David laughed. "And sometimes his left."

Her footsteps as she strode along with them faltered, and her face fell in horror as she looked up at Derek. "You have four hands?"

Derek grinned, and David's laughter echoed again. "With a sense of humor like that, you're going to fit right in," David told her, extending his hand in customary Earthly greeting. "Welcome on board."

She accepted his warm grasp with an uncertain smile.

"Research?" he asked.

"She likes dandelions," Derek answered.

David groaned but sent her a wink. "Sounds perfect!"

Passing through a set of glass doors and into a wide foyer, the three of them joined a parade of people walking purposefully in all directions. Signs with arrows and endless hallways seemed to lead everywhere, and Kristiana tried to read and look down each one. Hustled into a large office partitioned by a wall of smoky glass, she didn't have time to interpret or glimpse but a few before Derek and David stopped with her in front of a big wooden desk.

"Maggie Kirkpatrick, this is Kristiana Cooke," Derek announced, accepting a fistful of messages from his secretary. "Find her a job."

"Where?" the stout, gray-haired woman demanded, raising thick-lensed glasses to her nose to peer at Kristiana in frowning disapproval.

Kristiana retreated half a step under the intense glare, but, seemingly unaware of the exchange and already flipping through the slips of paper in his hand, Derek shrugged. "We just lost a mail clerk, didn't we? Put her there. She wants to learn all about the company. I can't think of a better place for her to start." He strode toward an open door that had his name emblazoned across it. "Oh, and get her a tetanus shot."

Left floundering under an unfriendly gaze, Kristiana suddenly found David's head next to her ear. "Don't let her scare you. Her bark is worse than her bite."

Trying to make sense of his words of wisdom, Kristiana could only swallow in trepidation as Maggie Kirkpatrick rose and, with an imperious gesture, ordered her to follow.

But if Maggie seemed unfriendly, everyone else was the opposite, and the fear that arose on being separated from Derek was quickly smothered.

From the company nurse to the mail-room supervisor, Kristiana was greeted by smiles and welcomes. While she'd never met so many Earthlings before, intimidation was quickly overcome by the warm acceptance of a firm built on the premise of profit sharing, all employees could own stock and everyone's opinion mattered. Whoever worked for Carpenter Pharmaceuticals had a say in what the company did, and the open policy promoted a relaxed atmosphere that encouraged mutual respect and cooperation.

Not given much time to acclimate or to adjust from one minute to the next, the worst part of the morning for Kristiana turned out to be the tetanus shot. The best, a tour of the entire facility. Accompanying a co-worker, Sandy Burke, on a mail run, Kristiana enjoyed being introduced around. Sandy was young and enthusiastic, and Kristiana not only returned her enthusiasm, but passed it on by asking as many questions of everyone she met as she could get in.

By lunch hour, her head was swimming with the possibilities of learning more about the manufacture and preparation of medicine, but even a trip to the basement cafeteria didn't give her a break to digest what she was learning. Letting Sandy select lunch for both of them, Kristiana sat down at a table with some researchers and tuned in to a debate on rain forest flora and fauna.

From across the room, Derek watched her.

Sitting at a table with David and some of the other company officers he could see his newest employee. Having been dumped without ceremony into a world of strangers, Kristiana seemed to be coping nicely. The animation on her face said she was enthralled by the rambling of one of his chief researchers, and it was clear from the attention she was getting that his chief was not the only one enjoying her.

Tendrils of unwanted jealousy wound into a knot in his stomach as he noticed the smiles directed at her from some of the company's younger men. Of course, it was hard to blame them for their admiration. In her form-fitting black jumpsuit, topped by one of his mother's blazers, Kristiana was striking. The bright red jacket highlighted the golden mass of hair flowing about her shoulders, and its unusual, near-white color seemed to say that not only it, but she, was special.

"About that new girl you hired," the mail-room supervisor said, plopping a tray unceremoniously onto Derek's table. "I think she has to go."

Derek's frown was immediate. "Why?"

"Because by the end of the day she's going to be running my department, and by the end of the week she's going to be running the company," the man said with a laugh.

"She asks a lot of questions," another supervisor chimed in. "Not dumb ones, either."

"Where'd you find her, anyway?" David asked.

"On the way home from Indiana. She was hitchhiking," Derek answered with a grin.

"No kidding!"

The roar of laughter and disbelief that followed carried to the other side of the lunchroom. Kristiana looked up to find herself caught by a glittering golden gaze. Derek was watching her. A flush of pleasure filled her, and the warmth of his quiet smile stayed with her through the afternoon as she retraced her steps along myriad corridors on the afternoon mail run and even when she returned to the distribution center to separate and sort the various correspondence and packages. Having fallen so unexpectedly to Earth, it was hard to imagine finding anyone who would have looked after her better or whom she would have preferred over him.

"Quitting time!" Sandy called when the hands on the clock hit five. She dove into her desk drawer for her purse. "Coming, Kristiana?"

"I must wait for a ride," she said with a shrug, her fingers full of papers she was arranging in alphabetical order.

"See you tomorrow, then!"

With her hands otherwise occupied, Kristiana could do little more than grin and call out goodbyes as others headed for the door. She was sure Derek would come for her when he was ready, but left alone, she saw no need to stop what she was doing, giving little thought to how comfortable she was as an employee of a company on Earth.

Her space travels had taken her to many places. She'd associated with various species and performed a multitude of tasks. She was used to adapting, but the job was always easier if she liked those she worked with. And she liked those at Carpenter Pharmaceuticals.

Getting one set of fingers free, she blindly reached for her discarded pencil, but it wasn't where she'd left it. Frowning, she began to search and saw that it had rolled just beyond her grasp. She looked back at the papers she was holding. To let them go would be to lose her order.

A quick glance around proved she was by herself. Everyone else who worked in the mail room was gone. Putting her hand out toward the pencil, she determined to make her brain work. Telekinesis wasn't such a difficult accomplishment. It was simply mind over matter. Roham did it all the time. Not big things, just small and he'd been helping her—with moderate success. He said she was just trying too hard.

Under her narrowed gaze, the pencil started to vibrate slightly. It was only a few inches away. Not far. It wouldn't take much effort.

COMING THROUGH the door, Derek's gaze swept the mail room in search of Kristiana. She wouldn't leave without him. Couldn't, unless she'd found a new place to stay. His mouth thinned at the idea. But then he spotted her at a far desk. And as he did, he would have sworn that the pencil she was reaching for jumped into her hand.

Startled, he blinked as she turned and began to write, unaware of his presence. He shook his head and put up a hand to rub his eyes. It had been a long day, and he'd done a lot of reading. Shrugging the perception away, he moved across the room. "What are you smiling at?"

Extremely pleased with herself for succeeding with the pencil, Kristiana jumped at the interruption and at nearly being caught using outworlder powers and the papers she'd been holding fell out of her grasp and back onto the cart. "Oh, no!"

Derek grinned. "Was it something I said?"

She looked woefully from the scattered sheets of paper to him. "I will have to sort them again in the morning."

"It'll keep you out of trouble," he told her, holding out his hand. "Come on. We've got things to do before then."

Out in the car and back on the road again, where the wild merging of vehicles was beginning in earnest once more, Kristiana braced herself for another rush hour and sought diversion in conversation. "Is it all right if I still stay with you?"

Derek glanced at her. "Why?"

"Sandy asked if I had a place to stay," Kristiana explained, hoping he wouldn't send her away. She didn't have long to remain on Earth—her rescuers could appear at any time—and she wanted to be with him. He made her feel safe—at least, most of the time. At others, any threat he posed had more to do with him being a man and her being a woman. "She has an extra room."

"What do *you* want to do?" he asked, his fingers tightening on the steering wheel.

She bit her lip. "I told her I had somewhere to sleep already."

"You didn't tell her you were living with me?"

"She did not ask."

"Then do not say," he advised, mimicking her lyrical way of speech with a teasing smile.

Kristiana frowned. "Why?"

"Gossip."

"It is a bad thing?"

"For you, it would be."

"Why not you, too?"

"I'm the boss."

Her frown deepened. "Bosses are not part of gossip?"

"They are, but they usually manage to rise above it even when they cause it."

"I do not think I understand."

"I hope you never have to." He glanced at her, again pondering her mix of innocence and wisdom. Where had she come from? Who was she really? His eyes darkened as he followed the flow of traffic forward. She wasn't ready to trust him with that yet, but he was determined she would be. Soon. "We're going to make a stop on the way home."

She turned interested eyes on him. Thus far her Earth experience had allowed her far more opportunities for exploration and shown her more about life on the planet than any of her people's previous, tenuous visits.

"We have to get you some more clothes."

"Clothes?"

"CLOTHES," he repeated a while later to a young saleswoman who eagerly came forward when he entered the store with Kristiana in tow. "For work and for play."

"Certainly," the clerk acknowledged, turning to Kristiana. "What size?"

"Size?" Kristiana asked, looking helplessly to Derek, who merely grinned and shook his head.

"I'll wait over here, out of earshot and out of the way."

But his move to save what he assumed was her vanity didn't help. His departure put the burden on the salesclerk to guess. But once figured out, Kristiana was swept into myriad designs, colors and fabrics. Changing from one outfit to another, she was enthusiastically caught up in experimenting with all the shades and styles.

Derek simply stood to the side and watched. "I think that will do it," he finally said. "Wrap those up for us please."

Kristiana, wearing what the saleswoman called designer jeans, T-shirt and a new pair of Nike, turned startled eyes on him. "We are taking *all* of these?"

"You don't like them?" Derek questioned with a raised brow.

"It is not that. It is just..." She watched the clerk begin bagging and boxing. She would never be able to wear everything he intended to buy during what she was beginning to regret would be too short a stay. Her wardrobe, from necessity and convenience, was normally limited. Biting her lower lip, she looked up at him. "There are so many, and the cost..." She didn't know much about Earth money, didn't understand the difference between designer and second-hand, didn't recognize the name of the store she stood in, nor could she appreciate the service she was getting any more than she totally comprehended the piece of plastic Derek presented for payment. Used to dealing in credits and trading and values accepted throughout the universe, she couldn't begin to compare Earth prices.

"Comes out of your first paycheck."

She looked at him suspiciously. "My work will pay for all of this?"

"It will all be paid for," Derek confirmed, but the dark look that came into his eyes didn't indicate that labor would be the charge. More likely, pleasure would satisfy the debt—for both of them.

Kristiana's knees trembled and heat stained her skin as he turned to sign the slip the salesclerk passed him, but silently—and shockingly, knowing it was forbidden—she found she couldn't wait for the work to begin.

Chapter Five

The smell of something cooking in the kitchen had Kristiana hurrying down the steps from her room, where she had been putting away the clothes from the store. The materials were unique and lovely to touch, especially the silk. It was disappointing to know she would have to leave all of it behind—with Derek.

Thoughts of him speeded her steps, and she grinned when she found him working at the stove. The future immediately disappeared from mind. The present was what mattered.

Still intimidated by the machinery in the room, she stuffed her hands into the pockets of her jeans and wandered over to stand beside him. She noted he, too, had changed into jeans and a T-shirt that left the well-toned muscles of his forearms bare.

He smiled as she leaned forward to stare down into the pan. "Stir-fry. Ever had it?"

She shook her head, not certain that she liked the scents bubbling up from the odd mixture in the pan.

"Shrimp, broccoli, carrots, pea pods, water chestnuts. You'll love it." She looked doubtful, so he picked a piece of broccoli from the plate beside him and held it out to her. "Open."

Faced with a green vegetable she'd never seen much less tasted before, she reluctantly opened her mouth to accept his offering. When her eyes lifted to his, the texture and flavor of the food was forgotten as she encountered his intense hazel gaze. Without warning the air between them charged. Gooseflesh rose on her arms, the breath caught in her chest, and her pulse jumped in alarm. She was standing so close to him, she could feel the heat of his body mingling with hers.

"How is it?" he managed to ask, though his thoughts weren't on the food. His grip on the utensil in his hand was so tight that his knuckles were white. He wanted to touch her.

Remembering suddenly to chew, she rolled the broccoli spear in her mouth and bit down to enjoy a mild taste with a crisp crunch. "I like it."

The puzzled relief in her voice made him laugh, breaking the tension between them. "Grab a couple of plates from the cupboard over there, and we'll go eat in front of the TV."

The meal was better than Kristiana had expected—many of the flavors of the various vegetables not unlike those on her own planet—but her attention was quickly diverted from eating by the television program Derek had turned on. "Star Trek: The Next Generation."

The story involved a humanoid captain who commanded a starship with a crew made up of beings from various planets. One member of the bridge was even an android, and the computers talked back when spoken to—just as hers did back home. The story was so real, the visual effects so stunning, she felt as if she had been transported into space with the crew of the USS *Enterprise*—and it was a space she knew and understood.

Trading, sharing, communicating between planets. Uneasy alliances, weapons that killed or stunned, peaceful commerce, orderly cities and all manner of natural wonders.

The program ended with a flash of the *Enterprise* warping into a galaxy of stars, and Kristiana sighed. It reminded her of home and space and of piloting a craft through the black velvet of stars, where danger, mystery and beauty coexisted.

"That was wonderful," she told Derek without looking away from the television. Such a show was the last thing she'd expected to see on Earth. Was the planet more ready for space travel than anyone on her world believed?

"You're a Trekker, too?"

She turned to find him watching the TV, and it was obvious he, too, had been caught up by the pictures that had flashed across the screen. "Trekker?"

He grinned. "Trekkers, Trekkies—diehard *Star Trek* fans." He gestured toward the television. "I've been one for years." He shook his head. "I think its appeal lies with the offer of hope. When you watch it, somehow you can believe that one day we'll actually do it."

"Travel to the stars?"

"That, and overcome all the problems that seem to be tearing the planet apart." He sighed. "Unity would be a nice thing to have instead of just talk about."

"It will not be easy." This she knew from experience and from her own people's history.

"But the benefits, the advances. Think of all the possibilities." His grin returned. "If I could, I'd catch the next space freighter out of here, wouldn't you?"

She looked back to the television screen, where the stars provided the backdrop for a series of credits as the majestic theme for the show filled the room, and thought of her brother, Roham. Had he gotten her message yet? When would he come for her? "I like their computer," she answered, blinking back the tears of loss that suddenly came to her eyes.

"Only because with one of those, you wouldn't have to cook."

Her gaze flew back to Derek's, and she found him smiling. "You are making fun of me."

Sitting beside her on the couch, he put out a hand to catch her chin in his fingers. He knew that touching her was something to avoid, but his action was automatic, his interest and desire to feel, acute. Since breaking up with Ann shortly after the death of his parents, he'd dated other women, but he was only now realizing how none of them had reached him. They hadn't stirred more than his hormones—perhaps because he hadn't allowed them to. But Kristiana moved him whether he wanted her to or not. "I'd never make fun of you."

She didn't resist when he pulled her closer, didn't object when his head lowered toward hers, even though she knew she should. He was from Earth. He might believe in fictional aliens, but was he ready to meet a real one? His lips blended with hers and she forgot interplanetary laws and taboos. Instead, a quiet sigh escaped her throat as she met his embrace. It was, after all, what she'd been waiting for.

Derek wasn't prepared for so complete a submission. He'd only wanted to test the waters, to discover if the chemistry boiling between them was real or a product of his imagination. But as she melted in his arms, fantasy was shattered, and he crushed her to him.

His hands slid from her back so that his fingers could bury themselves in the rich texture of her hair. It was like silk. His hands entangled in the thick, long strands as his mouth left hers to plunder her eyes, her face, her neck.

Kristiana was helpless under the assault.

Bending with his will, she pressed against him, enjoying his strength, his impatience, his passion. It matched hers. Following his lead, she traced the lines of his chest, the width of his shoulders and the lean power of his back. She opened her eyes and met the golden blaze burning in his. The color reminded her of where she was, of whom she was with, but she couldn't stop what she was doing. Knowing she was leaving, that she couldn't stay, only made her want to give more, be more, do more for him. She liked this man, and whether or not she was supposed to become involved with him, her affection was growing.

His mouth found hers again, but the shrill ring of the telephone jarred them apart. Derek determined to ignore it. He pulled her back once more, but the phone continued to ring. Insistent. Irritating. Demanding. He swore and swung away to grab the offending instrument. "Hello?"

The word was a snap, its harshness flicking off aroused nerve endings, and Kristiana watched him scowl.

"David?" Derek glanced at her. Her hair was a mess, the long strands tangled and tossed. He'd done that.

She watched his golden gaze flare and his hand reach out, but as she moved to accept it, he jerked his fingers back.

"What? Now?"

She frowned at his distress.

"They're at the airport? Why can't they wait until tomorrow to meet?"

She could feel his withdrawal, and it hurt even as she realized it was for the best.

"All right. Fine. I'll meet you there." He nodded. "Yes, I'm leaving now."

He slammed down the phone but didn't face her right away. Instead, he paused, as if gathering strength. Finally, he took a deep breath and turned to look at her. "I have to go. Some researchers we've been working with are at the airport. They've got a long layover before their flight leaves for Los Angeles. They want to meet with David and me to show us how the project's developing."

She nodded understanding as he rose to grab his jacket. The interruption had been timely. What had happened—what could have happened—between them wasn't right. Not for the two of them. Earth wasn't ready. She wasn't.

"I'll be back as soon as I can."

Watching him shrug into the waist-length coat, her heart skipped when she was again pinned by his stare. His eyes were full of promises—promises she couldn't allow him to keep. But abruptly he was turning away, striding out the door, and leaving her to struggle with her surging emotions.

Suddenly she found herself wishing her brother would hurry. The longer she stayed, the harder it would be to go. Her emotions were already reaching beyond herself, and she was growing too attached to the man who had rescued her. If her feelings got any stronger, leaving was an eventuality she would never survive.

"THANK YOU, KRISTY."

Kristiana smiled at the woman named Pat, accepted the mail from her hand, and pushed her cart forward toward the next desk. No one had ever called her by anything but her full name before, but she'd noticed that most Earthlings used abbreviated forms of their names. Pat was really Patricia. Sandy was actually Sandra. Kristiana accepted it as an odd type of compliment that she had been given a nickname, too. But the language still troubled her.

It wasn't that she couldn't understand the words said by those around her. It was the hidden meaning she sometimes couldn't grasp. Earth English was like no other language—and she knew many—she had ever encountered. Words not only had different spellings and meanings—such as *one* and *won*, or *to*, *two* and *too*— but even those with one spelling often had more than one definition.

A young male co-worker was particularly baffling in his speech. *Cool* was a word he used often, but while *she* thought it meant *cold*, he seemed to believe it described something good. And when he used *awesome*, he wasn't speaking of reverence or wonder but rather of something he found incredible. It was quite confusing, but if she was slow to catch on, nobody seemed to hold it against her.

The executive offices of Carpenter Pharmaceuticals loomed ahead as she wheeled her cart into the hall, and Kristiana felt her heartbeat accelerate against her ribs. Derek was working somewhere behind the smoky glass.

The night before she had been in bed when he'd returned from his meeting. She'd lain listening as his footsteps had seemed to hesitate in the hall, but he hadn't tested the door that she'd purposely left unlocked. He'd gone to his own room without attempting to bother her. And this morning, when they'd shared breakfast before driving to work, he'd made no mention of their embrace the evening before. Perhaps, for his own reasons, he, too, was regretting the impulse that had driven them into each other's arms.

Reaching and accepting Maggie Kirkpatrick's packet of mail, Kristiana was glad she didn't have to smile or form a friendly greeting. Her heart was too heavy, knowing she'd somehow disappointed the man who had saved her from capture. But as she turned to leave Maggie's desk, her fears abruptly returned. Walking through the door were two men: one dark, and somber, the other, young and tall, with bright red hair. She recognized them as the investigators she'd seen on television examining her spaceship. They had found her!

BEHIND HIS CLOSED DOOR, Derek frowned at the papers he'd been trying to read but had been unable to focus on for the past hour. His inability to concentrate was annoying. His lack of control was infuriating.

Shoving the papers aside, he threw his pen down and sat back in his big, cushioned chair to stare at the ceiling. It was ridiculous that Kristiana could so interrupt his routine. He barely knew her. She was a stranger. A strange stranger, at that. But he couldn't stop thinking about her. She fascinated, intrigued and unintentionally taunted him.

He sighed. The outburst of passion on the couch after dinner last night hadn't been her doing. He scowled. It hadn't been his, either. What it had been was spontaneous combustion—a problem he'd never had to such a degree before. Not even with Ann.

His brow furrowed in thought. The attraction that had brought Ann and him together had been quietly exciting, arousing, without consuming. Since their separation, he'd limited his relationships. Given in to desire. Simple lust. But he'd cut himself off from any deeper emotions. Unconsciously, he hadn't been willing to risk failure—or loss—again.

His mother had worried for him as a boy because he felt things so strongly, had allowed passion to overrule sense. Age and maturity had allowed him to recognize and manage that part of himself. Derek sighed. Unfortunately, without his being aware of it, he had also buried the need to feel, to care, to share with another person—because of the pain commitment sometimes involved. Kristiana had somehow unearthed those emotions. She'd loosened the restraints he'd unwittingly tied himself in. She'd managed to make him want to try—even at the risk of being hurt—again.

The possibility existed for the two of them. The chemistry was there. The universal magic of man and woman blending constantly bubbled just below the surface whenever they were together. He not only wanted her. He enjoyed her, too.

She was an intriguing mix of intelligence and simplicity, wisdom and innocence. It was in her eyes, in her actions. The contrasts both appealed and alarmed. He wanted to possess and protect her at the same time.

Swearing, he grabbed the papers from his desk. How was he supposed to do both? She trusted him, yet he'd nearly seduced her on his couch. His gaze rose, and he stared, unseeing, into space. Still, she hadn't exactly fought off his advances, and she hadn't seemed intimidated this morning. But she had been quiet. His frown returned. Tonight they were going to talk.

The buzzer on his desk sounded, and he reached to flick on the intercom. "Yes, what is it?"

"There are two government agents here to see you, Mr. Carpenter."

His frown of annoyance turned to one of curiosity. "Government? Send them in." Releasing the button, he tossed the papers aside and rose to greet the two men who were already coming through the door. Derek extended his hand. "Gentlemen."

"Ron Rogers," the first man said, returning the handshake. He was of medium height, dark, and nondescript. He could blend into any crowd anywhere. His partner was another story. Young, red-haired and as thin as he was tall, he would be difficult not to notice wherever he went.

"Tony Magrini," the redhead offered as Derek shook his hand.

"I'd introduce myself, but I'm sure you know who I am or you wouldn't be here." Derek smiled and motioned to the chairs in front of his desk before returning to stand behind it. "So haven't I been paying enough taxes?"

Rogers laughed as he took a seat. "Nothing so drastic. We're just following up on a credit card charge you made on Saturday night."

Derek leaned forward to accept a slip of paper from Rogers. He recognized the signature on it immediately. It was his. He stared at the date and the logo of a gas station.

"Saturday I was driving back from Indiana. It was late. I didn't get home until early Sunday." He shrugged and handed the credit slip back. "I stopped more than once to fill up."

"This would have been about midnight," Rogers told him as Derek sank into the chair behind his desk. "And you may have noticed something unusual at about that time. A bright flash of light across the sky, perhaps?"

Derek's grin was instantaneous. "The satellite that crashed?" He nodded. "I saw it, all right. Bigger and better than any shooting star I've ever seen."

"You were at the station when it passed over?" Rogers queried.

"No, it was just before I pulled into the station that I saw it go by overhead. Lit up the countryside for miles." His lips twisted with amusement. "I don't imagine NASA is too thrilled."

Rogers laughed and Magrini smiled. "Their satellites *are* rather expensive," Rogers agreed.

Derek looked from one man to the other. "So, what is it I can do for you? I'm afraid I'm not in the business of launching things into outer space or catching them when they fall."

Magrini shook his head. "We were just wondering if you saw anything else unusual that night."

Derek frowned. "Like what?"

"Could you describe for us exactly what you saw?" Rogers asked. "For the record."

Derek shrugged as he watched him pull a notebook and pencil from his pocket. "Not much to tell, really. As I said, I was going down the road, this flash of light streaked across the sky, and the last I saw of it was when it disappeared over a hill."

"Did you hear it crash?"

Derek blinked in surprise at Magrini who'd asked the question. Up until that moment he hadn't thought about any sound the object had made, just its brightness. But, as big as it had to have been, if it had crashed, he certainly should have heard as well as seen it. Everyone for miles around would have. He frowned in reflection. "Actually, no, but I did have the windows rolled up."

"There was only one object?" Rogers asked, making a note on his pad.

Derek took a deep breath as he thought back on that night.

"No smaller objects by it, falling from it, following it?" Rogers clarified.

"No, it seemed to be in one piece..." Suddenly Derek wondered if they were talking about simple debris from a damaged satellite. Smaller objects "by" or "falling from" it? How could a crashing satellite be "followed"? With the pull of gravity and the uncertainty of a decaying orbit that would surely see the device either break up or melt upon reentry into the earth's atmosphere, any debris would have been particlized at best, making accurate tracking impossible. Unless... Derek's suspicions increased as he looked from one man to the other.

"Did you see anyone else in the area after your sighting?" Rogers pressed. "Besides the gas station attendant?"

Denial was almost immediate. The gas station had been empty. No one else had been there.

Except Kristiana.

His stomach flipped. Unbeknownst to him, she had been hiding in his back seat. How had she gotten there? Where had she come from?

Suddenly dizzy, Derek shoved to his feet and began to pace, acting as if he were trying to remember. And he *was* remembering, but not what they wanted him to. What was it she'd said when he'd shown her the aloe plant?

Do you think that's true on every planet?

And what of her reaction to seeing the fallen satellite on the news? How still, almost frightened, she'd seemed? And what about her inability to operate something as simple as a toaster...? He shook his head in disbelief. He was going mad. What he was thinking wasn't possible.

"Mr. Carpenter?"

Derek turned to look at the two men, and abruptly realized anything was possible. "I'm sorry, I was trying to recall if I'd seen any other cars. I know I passed at least one, but I think that was before I reached the station." He shook his head and exercised the composure he'd mastered from years of negotiations across a conference table. "No one was at the station except the attendant—unless there was someone inside. I didn't go in. Didn't use a rest room. And when I left..." He held out his hands, helplessly. "I don't remember seeing any other cars. The highway was pretty empty that night— except for a deer. I almost hit a doe."

"Lucky you missed," Rogers said, and snapped his notebook shut. "Could have totaled your car."

Derek gestured helplessly again, but his mind was still whirling. If Kristiana was... If these men found out about her... The urge to guard and protect her rushed forward. "I'm sorry, but I just don't recall seeing anyone else that night."

"No hitchhikers?" Magrini asked, a hopeful note creeping into his voice.

Derek grinned. "If there were, I didn't see them. I was pretty tired. I probably shouldn't even have driven home that night."

"We appreciate your time, Mr. Carpenter," Rogers said, rolling to his feet and digging into his pocket. "If you do remember anything else about that night, we'd appreciate your giving us a call."

Derek accepted a business card and quickly examined it.

"That number will get you through to me at any time."

Derek followed them to the door, speaking only as Magrini's hand settled on the knob. "It seems strange that the government is spending so much time investigating a downed satellite."

Both government agents turned.

"Don't you think?" Derek asked with a smile that somehow belied the innocent tone of the question.

"As we agreed," Rogers answered smoothly, "satellites are expensive."

"But once they're destroyed, useless." Derek shook his head and looked from one man to the other. "All this effort could cause someone to speculate that your search was for—" he smiled "—a who rather than a what."

Chapter Six

"You mean, like little green men, perhaps?" Rogers abruptly laughed.

Derek laughed, too. "Something like that."

"If something—or someone—besides a satellite hit Earth, Mr. Carpenter, I assure you that the U.S. Government would send out more than two people to investigate."

Derek grinned at Rogers. "Who says you're the only two out looking?" He raised his eyebrows in inquiry as their smiles faded and they fell grimly silent. Walking away, he moved toward his desk. "It'd be interesting to call my congressman—we're good friends, you know—to get the whole story. Unless, of course, you'd like to tell me. Because somehow the possibility that I'd seen a downed satellite just doesn't seem to me to warrant so much attention that you'd actually track me down through a credit card charge."

Rogers and Magrini maintained their silence as Derek sat down again behind his desk.

"Yes, invasion of privacy, violation of my constitutional rights. I think I have a right to know why I'm being investigated, don't you?"

Neither government agent spoke. They remained still, and moments ticked quietly past until, finally, Rogers and Magrini turned away from Derek's steady gaze to exchange a troubled look.

"If you're worried about my security clearance," Derek offered, "you may remember Agent Orange and Desert Storm. This company's been trying to find cures for the ills our government and Saddam Hussein created. The higher-ups in Washington are pretty picky about who knows how much regarding certain top-secret efforts."

"Yes, they are," Rogers was quick to agree. "*Very* picky."

Derek grinned and continued as if Rogers hadn't spoken. "Seeing as I'm already part of the government's exclusive network of know-it-alls, where's the harm in my being included on this particular secret?"

"We didn't say anything about a secret," Magrini objected, the color in his face heightening to match the red of his hair.

"You didn't have to." Derek shrugged. "You just had to show up here."

Rogers shoved his suit coat aside and stuffed his hands into the pockets of his pants before slowly returning to stand beside a chair in front of the desk. "We're investigating the possibility that an unidentified flying object crash-landed outside Chicago."

"A UFO. Not a satellite," Derek said more than asked.

"We can't tell you anything else," Magrini snapped, clearly uncomfortable with his partner's decision to talk.

"Can't or won't?" Derek countered as he turned back to Rogers.

"What crashed wasn't one of ours," Rogers responded after a slight hesitation. "It didn't come from anywhere on Earth. Or, at least, nobody's admitting that it did."

"A spaceship?"

Rogers shrugged, turning again toward the door. "It was a burned-out hulk by the time it hit."

"But it didn't *hit*," Derek corrected, successfully stopping the agents as they tried once more to leave. "It landed. No crash." He nodded as the two men exchanged sharp glances. "During the newscast, I didn't think about it, but the grass wasn't burned and the ground wasn't broken. If the ship had crashed, the impact would have driven it into the dirt. There would have been a crater around the craft caused by the impact. But the earth wasn't disturbed. It was only slightly blackened." He abruptly remembered Kristiana's arm. The cut, the burn. Had she been trapped inside? He swallowed and kept his expression neutral. "You think someone inside got out." It was a statement, not a question.

Magrini came striding forward from where he'd lingered by the door. His hope of escaping with as little breach of confidence as possible was forgotten, and his face under his red hair had brightened even more. "Why would you say some*one* and not some*thing*?"

Derek shrugged. "Some*thing* would have received a lot more attention—publicity, even—I would think. But a humanoid presence . . ." He studied the straight faces in front of him. "You found something at the site."

Rogers and Magrini again exchanged unwilling glances.

Derek shoved himself to his feet. "Come on, gentlemen. I was just discussing with a friend last night the possibilities of space travel. Just because we can't do it doesn't mean anybody else out there can't. It's a big universe. We're only kidding ourselves if we think we're alone in it.''

"Footprints," Rogers reluctantly conceded. "Leaving the site."

Derek frowned. "But how can you be sure they were made by someone who was inside the ship? What about all the people coming to roam the area after the crash?''

"It was late at night. Hardly anyone saw it," Magrini objected. "Almost immediately after discovery, the police roped off the area for safety's sake because of the heat and smoke. They didn't want anyone getting hurt.''

"And only one pair of footprints headed directly away from the craft in the opposite direction of the road or any habitation," Rogers added.

"Surely you followed them," Derek protested. "Tracked..."

"Why do you think we're here?"

Magrini's question stopped Derek.

"The prints were small, humanlike—a booted foot," Magrini continued. "At first, the direction was straight, and fast, but a short distance later the tracks became random, slow, and uncertain. As if, after escape, whoever it was couldn't make up their mind as to where to go.''

"But then," Rogers said, leaning a hip against the desk, "came the gas station you stopped at. In the dead of night, with no other lights or buildings around, it would have been easy to spot the station from one of the hills surrounding the crash site.''

"The station attendant..." Derek prompted.

"Didn't see a thing," Rogers answered. But his partner didn't seem convinced of that.

"He swears he was alone all night, except for customers, and that he saw nothing unusual." Magrini grumbled. "Says he didn't even see the lights when the craft passed overhead."

"The footprints disappeared there?" Derek asked, remembering Kristiana huddled in the back seat of his car. Both men nodded confirmation and he took a deep breath to steady himself. Her footprints would have stopped as soon as she'd stepped onto the concrete surrounding the gas station. His attention returned to the agents. The need to protect her forced him to ask, "That's all you have? No other leads?"

"Just what one man swears he saw."

Derek held his breath as he stared at Rogers.

"Someone in black with white hair running away from the craft."

Any doubts vanished. Silently releasing the air from his lungs, Derek turned his back on the agents to stare out the window and hide the impact of revelation. Kristiana wasn't from Earth! An alien. She was an alien! "Incredible," he managed to murmur.

"That's why we asked if you'd seen any other objects in the sky. We were thinking the craft may have been followed by another," Rogers explained. "But all of this we're telling you . . ."

"Is confidential." Derek turned from the window, looking, no doubt, exactly what he was—amazed, unsure, shocked, excited. And afraid—for her. "I wish you luck on the hunt, gentlemen. I'm sorry I couldn't be of more help—or tell you that I've had an encounter of the third kind."

"So are we," Rogers grunted, studying Derek as he spoke. "We were never here, of course."

"Never, but I wish you could let me know if—"

Rogers cut him off. "I think we've pushed the boundaries of discretion enough already."

Derek nodded. "Understood. Reluctantly."

"You can always call your congressman," Magrini suggested, following Rogers to the door. "The one you're such good friends with."

Derek grinned. "I've never even met him."

Rogers and Magrini both stopped dead in their tracks. Their expressions reflected their incredulity at having been outmaneuvered.

"Have a nice day, gentlemen." Derek's satisfied smile remained in place until the door closed behind them. Once alone, his composure crumbled. "My God..." He moved numbly to the window and saw, in his mind, scene after scene of Kristiana since he'd met her, recognizing the uniqueness, finally understanding the innocent wisdom, the hesitant actions, the earnest attempts to express and comprehend.

It was almost too much to take in. Possibilities and questions buzzed in his brain, but suddenly fear overtook all else. They were looking for her. He had to let her know. Even as he started to turn, he realized there was no need. She wouldn't have been running if she hadn't known she would be followed. Still, she didn't know they were this close. He turned toward the door, and she was there.

Seeming to have materialized out of nowhere, Kristiana stood in the middle of his office watching him. As his heart thudded in surprised alarm, he was tempted to believe she had appeared out of thin air. But he'd felt her flesh. It was warm and solid and... human.

"It's you they're looking for, isn't it?"

His words were quiet, but he didn't seem to be afraid, even though she was. When she'd first seen the men, anxiety had nearly driven her to run. When they had walked past her as if she didn't exist, she'd stayed and waited and worried. Derek had protected her once. Would he do so again?

And after he realized who—what—she was, how would he look at her? As a friend? A woman? An alien invader? She didn't want him to hate her. Fear her. He'd been kind. He'd been ... more than she'd expected.

With her gaze locked on his, she searched his eyes. They were calm. Clear. He wasn't running away, but he wasn't coming closer, either. Rejection was a painful thing. She nodded. "You did not tell them about me."

"Didn't," he corrected. "You have to learn to use contractions more. People will notice if you don't. I did."

"I am—I'm trying. Sometimes it ... it's difficult."

"English isn't an easy language to learn." He stared at her, trying to see the difference, the something that would show her to be what she was—an alien from outer space, but he couldn't spot it. To him, she was merely a woman. A beautiful woman standing in the middle of his office with the sun shining through the windows forming a halo around the golden-white mass of hair that hung rich and free around her shoulders.

He still wanted her.

It didn't matter where she was from.

Yet as he watched her, and she him, he suddenly sensed the unexpected. Fear. She was afraid. Of him. Of what he could do.

"They wanted to know if I'd seen anything besides the crash. I told them no."

She couldn't stop the shudder of relief that shook her.

"But they are looking for you. For someone. They found footprints leaving the...your ship, and someone saw you running away." He saw her eyes widen and her body tense. "Not enough to identify you as man or woman. Just someone in black, with white hair, running from the site."

She lifted a hand to the offending mass of whitish gold.

Recognizing her uncertainty, Derek hastened to reassure her. "They have no real leads. You're safe."

Some of her tension drained away and left Kristiana feeling weak.

Taking a tentative step forward, away from the windows and toward her, he thought her posture was not unlike that of the doe's he'd seen in the road the night he'd found her. Poised, ready to flee if need be. "I have so many questions. I don't know where to begin."

She nodded understanding. "I will try to answer."

Derek stopped at his desk, wanting to go to her, to touch her, to hold her, and offer comfort and support, but he was uncertain if that was acceptable behavior—for someone not of Earth. "How... Why are you here?"

"My ship," she said with an apologetic shrug. "The controls malfunctioned. I was spinning."

"But you managed to land."

"Yes, but the screening device was not—wasn't working. Anyone watching would have seen the ship enter your atmosphere." She shivered as she remembered the shuddering, bucking craft, the flames shooting out of the panels, the smoke. "I was fortunate to escape."

"But you were hurt."

She unconsciously raised a hand to her arm. "There was a fire." She shook her head. "I was able to get out and start the self-destruct mechanism, but it did not—didn't," she corrected herself again, "work."

Derek remembered the newscast. "When you saw the ship on television . . ."

Kristiana nodded. "An explosion inside the ship should have destroyed everything, but it did not."

"They can't have found much," he hastened to console her.

"No." The word was filled with defeat, and she looked suddenly tired.

He took another step forward. "What will happen now? Are you stranded?" He couldn't imagine it. The terror of being alone, completely and totally alone, where nothing and no one was familiar—not even, he abruptly realized, the food you ate.

"They will come." Hope gleamed in the blue eyes she raised to him.

"They?"

"Roham. He will come when my message reaches the mother ship."

"Mother . . ." Derek lifted a hand to drag it through his hair, feeling overwhelmed. "How many of you are there?"

She shrugged. "We are a trading expedition. Not many."

"And you've been to Earth before?"

"I have, only once. Roham has been here three times." Her fingers linked in front of her, her gaze dropped. "Earth is not a place to visit often. It is dangerous. You are not ready."

Derek remembered the classic movie *The Day The Earth Stood Still.* They'd shot that emissary from space.

But in *Close Encounters of the Third Kind,* the greeting had been hopeful, eager—for some at least. Those not consumed with fear of the unknown. "Then why do you come at all?"

"To follow your progress. We are waiting for a time when you *will* be ready. And because we are curious."

He smiled. "We have that in common at least."

His smile warmed her, and her lips curved in response. "You are much like us."

Unconsciously, his steps continued to carry him slowly forward. "Who are 'us'? Where are you from?"

She bit her lip. "I am not sure what you call it, but we call my home Takyam."

"In the Milky Way?"

She shook her head and shrugged in seeming embarrassment. "We do not call it the Milky Way."

He laughed and shoved his hands into his pockets as he stopped in front of her. "Yes, it's rather arrogant of us to believe we can name whatever we see from our world and expect everyone else in the universe to call it the same thing." His eyes searched hers. "What do you call Earth?"

She shrugged. "Earth, because that is what you call it."

"And before you knew what we called it?"

"I do no—don't," she corrected herself again, "remember. We have called it Earth since before I was born."

Awed, he shook his head. "You've been traveling in space that long?"

"Of necessity."

"I don't understand."

"Takyam is not really a planet, but a moon. It revolves with three other moons around a planet we call

Kazanbar, which is much like your Jupiter. My home world is not as self-sufficient as Earth. None of the moons are. When we first realized our resources were dwindling, space was our only hope of survival. We used everything we had to reach other worlds to begin exploration."

"And you made contact."

"With the other moons and their inhabitants," she agreed, but sighed. "At first what was needed was taken by war. But eventually we all realized that peace could provide us with the same result without bloodshed and even increase the amount of material available for our use. An alliance was formed, and we learned to trade."

"And explored the galaxy together."

She smiled at his enthusiasm, but it was a sad expression. "Do not think we are a superior race, or all is well in the galaxies beyond. People do not always get along. In some places there is not enough food. Some planets will not join the alliance. Our world has a better balanced society than your Earth, but only because we have had to make it so. We learned how to share and to live together to continue to survive. Yet by being more technically advanced and achieving intergalactic travel, we are not better than those on Earth. Your knowledge is beyond ours in areas other than space exploration."

He remembered the dandelions. "Medicine."

Her eyes darkened with unspoken sorrow. "The boy I told you of who lost his leg has a wooden stump for a limb, lives with pain each day. People die from a simple cut or what you would call a common cold."

"But, research . . ."

''We try learning from others, but many in our galaxy are like us. The rush for survival by trading in space takes priority over saving lives. The building of satellites, spacecrafts and space stations comes before discovering how to heal illness or injury, because to fall behind means to be left behind—or be invaded by those who have not yet joined the alliance.''

''Not unlike the universe set out in *Star Trek*. They, too, encounter enemies.''

''Yes, but it is getting better. Ties and time bring change, and trade brings union between races along with better understanding. Once we are strong enough and sure enough of one another, our attention can turn back to the needs of daily living.''

He nodded, unconsciously still searching for something that would show him she wasn't anything like other women he knew. ''The other moons. The people. Are they like you?''

''All are humanoid,'' she told him, a soft flush filling her cheeks under his steady gaze. ''On Takyam we all have my coloring. On another moon they are dark rather than light. On another, because of the difference in atmosphere, the ears are bigger and the faces flatter. Stronger gravity on the last, makes bodies broader and heavier.''

''You said there are unions between races. You... mate with each other?''

Suddenly breathless as his eyes remained warm on hers, she remembered the feel of his arms around her. No man from any planet or moon had ever moved her as this one from Earth did. ''It is not uncommon.''

He started to pull a hand from his pocket but suddenly stopped. The need to touch was still there, but now, more than before, he questioned the rightness of it. Etiquette. Manners. What was the proper code of behavior when faced with someone from outer space? "You're . . . Are you married? Do you marry?"

She smiled as he stumbled for words. "I am **as** you are, without a mate, but Roham is . . ." She searched for the Earth word.

"Engaged?"

Another word with dual meanings. She shrugged. "He will take a wife soon. Our customs are not unlike yours."

"I'm glad to hear it." His grin was silly, infectious. It made her laugh, but as he watched, her blue eyes darkened.

"I must go."

His hands shot out of his pockets to grab her shoulders. "No!" Just as quickly, he let her go. "I'm sorry. I didn't mean . . . there's no need for you to leave. At least not until your brother comes."

"But . ."

"They won't look for you here anymore."

"You will not be . . . uncomfortable?"

Looking into the warm blue of her gaze, feeling the pull of an attraction he was trying hard to deny—especially given the circumstances, he remembered the couch and the embrace, and shook his head. Where she was from didn't matter. Her being from another planet didn't change his feelings. "Not at all."

"I would like to stay." The way he was staring at her made her wish she'd never have to leave.

"I'd," he corrected. "Contractions."

"I'd." She stood gazing up at him. "You could teach me many things."

More than she wanted to know, he was sure, and the muscles in his stomach tightened.

She reached out to take his hand and smiled shyly up at him. ''You wish to mate with me.''

Chapter Seven

Derek's jaw dropped, and his fingers jumped in hers. "I..."

"It is what you are thinking," she told him, "is it not?"

"I..." His eyes widened in alarm. "Can you read my mind?"

Her grin was childlike. "Sometimes, when people open themselves to me."

Self-preservation had him pulling his hand from hers. "This is the first time? Since you met me?"

She made a face. "Yes. I am not very good at telepathy. I am sorry."

"I'm," he corrected automatically and tried to hide his relief. "And don't be sorry." He shook his head. "I think having my mind read is something I'd have to get used to."

"It is not very common. Telepathy is something only some of my people are beginning to use regularly, but there are those on other worlds who communicate by thought, not words, all the time." She shuddered. "It can be unsettling."

"To say the least," Derek adamantly agreed.

Recognizing his discomfort, she hurried to apologize. "I did not mean to upset you."

"No, don't. It's . . . all right."

"No, it is not polite to invite yourself into another's mind."

"Invite . . ."

"My people, most of them, have some type of . . ." She struggled to explain. "Special mental abilities. It is a trait in our race that seems to have become stronger in us as we have accepted differences among us—for example, that some have always been able to use their minds for more than pure thought."

Derek frowned. "We have a few on Earth with such abilities—ESP, teleportation, telekinesis—but they're usually regarded as freaks or frauds."

"We felt much the same until visits to other worlds showed us that such mental abilities can be quite common, but we still have much to learn."

He frowned. "I thought I saw you move a pencil without using your hands the other day, but I put it down to my imagination."

Her eyes darkened with guilt and dropped. "I was afraid you had." She shrugged in apology. "Roham is much better at moving things with his mind. I am slower to learn."

Awe filled her voice and his mind. "The dog . . ."

She smiled. "I told you that you could learn to understand him, too."

Derek shook his head in denial, but the possibility was intriguing. Suddenly, with her, he wanted to try. "Maybe you can teach me, too." His eyes and hands caught hers. "How long can you stay? When will Roham come?"

She lifted her shoulders in a helpless shrug. "I cannot be certain."

Derek smiled a little sadly. "Then we'll have to enjoy what time we have. How about a celebration tonight? I've never had an encounter of the third kind before."

She frowned in confusion. "How many kinds of encounters are there?"

His hand found her cheek. "More than I've probably ever imagined."

SEATED ACROSS from Derek in a restaurant hours later, Kristiana watched him pour liquid from a bottle into shallow glasses. Before coming to find something to eat, he'd taken her home so they could change clothes. She was now wearing a dress of sky blue with a tight bodice, draped sleeves and a full skirt. The material was pretty and comfortable against her skin, but the shoes... With high heels that made it hard to balance when she walked, the footwear pinched her toes. Beneath the table, she slipped the elegant shoes off to rub her bare feet together as Derek handed her a glass.

"Champagne," he told her. "To celebrate."

She smiled and brought the glass to her lips. "It has bubbles." She laughed as they tickled her nose. "This is a common drink?"

"For happy times."

"I am glad you are happy," she assured him, and watched as he clinked his glass gently against hers.

"To new acquaintances."

His smile warmed her even as the drink she sipped did. The liquid raced down her throat to settle in her stomach with a comfortable glow. "It is very good," she assured him and drank again. "Almost like Harbisian ale."

"But not like anything on Takyam?"

She wrinkled her nose. "Perhaps biscal?"

His eyes caught hers. "I wish I could taste it."

Without his saying the words, she knew what he meant. Their time together would be all too short. She would leave soon, and he would remain behind. Her gaze darkened on his. "I, too."

Catching her fingers with his, he suddenly found himself never wanting to let go. "Perhaps we'll meet again. Earth might make it into space in my lifetime."

But he doubted it.

And so did she. Yet she wanted to believe, and tightened her grip in his. "Perhaps," she agreed.

"Derek! What a surprise!"

Automatically turning to stand at the greeting, Derek cringed inwardly as his hand was grasped in the bearlike paw of a barrel-chested man. "Tom Patterson," he greeted with a smile, silently praying, just once, that this conversation with the executive of a competitive pharmaceutical company would be short.

"Out for dinner?" Patterson asked, extending his smile to Kristiana. "You don't mind if we join you for a moment, do you?"

An objection formed on Derek's lips, but he wasn't given a chance to voice it. Patterson sat down and dragged a woman forward to take the chair beside him.

"Tom Patterson," he offered, holding out a hand to Kristiana. "And this is my wife, Beth."

Left with no choice, Derek swallowed a sigh and took his seat, keeping his tone polite, resolving that Patterson's stay would be brief. "Kristiana Cooke," he said, completing the introductions.

Kristiana smiled in greeting, any disappointment she felt at the interruption lost as her curiosity was aroused by the sequined gown Beth Patterson wore. Bright and red and in poor taste for a simple cocktail outfit, it had an outlandish gaudiness that attracted Kristiana's untutored gaze. "Your dress is beautiful."

"Why, thank you," Beth Patterson gushed, and as her husband captured Derek in a nonstop marathon of business babble, she launched into a steady rundown of current fashions and of all the "in" stores from Chicago to Paris.

It was quite beyond Kristiana's comprehension. The woman's words came fast and furious, their meaning mostly lost. Kristiana simply stopped trying to focus on what was being said and concentrated instead on Beth Patterson's animated gestures, mannerisms and heavy makeup. Kristiana was certain she'd never seen anyone anywhere with redder lips.

She drained her glass of champagne as Beth took a gasp of air. "This is very good," she offered.

"Champagne?" Beth asked. "It's one of my favorites."

"We're celebrating," Derek put in, using the opportunity to break away from Patterson to refill Kristiana's glass. "We just met."

The hint was lost on both Pattersons as each started anew on conversations they monopolized, but Kristiana didn't mind. Not having to think or speak, she could sit and enjoy the beverage that was beginning to make her a bit light-headed. It was a pleasant sensation. She held her glass out to Derek for another refill.

"It is very good," she repeated, and watched him splash more into her glass.

"It's better to drink this slowly," he cautioned. "It can hit you quickly."

"You're right," Beth heartily agreed. "I remember when..."

Derek tuned out both her and her husband as Kristiana raised the glass to her lips again. Her hand was steady, her gaze clear, but he was beginning to wonder if mixing champagne and aliens was a good idea. After all, he didn't know what, if any, tolerance she would have for alcohol. His concern was abruptly justified when she started to giggle.

"This is very good," she repeated yet again.

"And you've probably had enough," Derek told her, and took the drained glass from her hand, not influenced at all by the pout she directed at him. He was more interested in getting rid of Patterson and his wife so he could give Kristiana his undivided attention. If he could rush them on their way, the evening could still be saved.

"Where are you from?" Patterson unexpectedly asked Kristiana.

"Yes," Beth agreed. "You have such a lovely accent."

Kristiana's smile was both gracious and brilliant. "Takyam."

Derek nearly spit out his drink.

"I've never heard of it," Patterson said with a frown.

"It's in Wyoming," Derek clarified loudly with a meaningful glance at Kristiana, but she just smiled and shook her head.

"No, it is a light-year beyond Pluto."

Patterson laughed heartily. "On the other side of the Milky Way, right?"

Beth tittered happily. "So silly to name a bunch of stars after a candy bar, don't you think?"

Kristiana turned puzzled, slightly clouded eyes on Derek. "You have named the stars after candy?"

"Not exactly," Derek said, standing. It was definitely time to end the conversation. "Listen, Tom," he said, extending his hand and drawing the big man from his chair, "why don't you give me a call tomorrow to go over this?"

The discussion was lost on Kristiana as her attention dropped from Derek to his deserted champagne glass. It was full yet. With a smile, she pointed a finger and brought it across the table to her with a thought.

Beth gasped. "Do you know magic?"

"Magic," Kristiana agreed. The champagne made her feel warm and happy and light as a feather. She put Derek's glass to her lips. He wouldn't mind if she drank his, too.

With his back to the table, Derek was about to turn around to hasten Beth Patterson on her way with her husband when he, along with everyone else in the restaurant, heard her squeal.

"Tom! Look at this!"

Derek swung with Patterson and felt his stomach plummet, then jolt in alarm. For, twirling through the air above the table was every glass, plate and piece of silverware that had been laid out on it. Kristiana had them spinning in happy circles above the white tablecloth. Without turning, Derek heard the murmurs behind and around him, and fear had his throat closing. Extra attention was not what Kristiana needed. As Patterson opened his mouth to speak, Derek quickly stepped forward with a forced laugh. "Showing off again, Kristiana? She's a magician's apprentice, you know."

Beth clapped. "I just love magic!"

Derek slid into the chair beside Kristiana. "Yes, so does she." Beneath the table, he took her hand and squeezed it tightly. "Time to put everything down, Kristiana. You're distracting everyone from their dinner."

As soon as he touched her, she lost her concentration, turned to smile at him, and everything dropped. China, crystal and silverware came down with a crash. Champagne splattered, glass broke, and forks and spoons clanged together in a discordant chorus. Kristiana put a hand over her mouth in surprised wonder at the ensuing mess. "Roham would be most unhappy with me."

Feeling every eye in the room on them, Derek gritted his teeth. "*I'm* unhappy with you," he growled beneath his breath, but he smiled at Patterson and his wife. "I'm afraid she's had a bit too much to drink. I'd better take her home." Not giving anyone a chance to reply, he grabbed Kristiana's hand and pulled her to her feet. "Tomorrow, Tom."

Kristiana stumbled after him, oblivious to the stares and snickers and shaking heads, but as she reached the door, she realized something was missing. "My shoes!"

Derek looked down at her bare feet and swore under his breath. "Forget them!"

Swept into his arms and tossed over his shoulder, Kristiana suddenly found herself viewing the parking lot upside down, but the numbing effect of the champagne stopped her from feeling any discomfort. "We are not having dinner?"

"Not if you can't behave yourself," Derek retorted, weaving toward his sedan through the sea of parked cars outside the restaurant.

"Does that mean we will have no more champagne?"

"I think you've had enough."

"It is very good."

"So you keep telling me." He set her down and put out a steadying hand when she weaved uncertainly in front of him.

"I feel dizzy." She put a hand to her head. "Everything is moving."

"Champagne will do that to you," he mused, unlocking the door and guiding her into the passenger seat. "Just sit back and relax."

Kristiana did as she was told as he walked around the car to the driver's side, but she was horrified to see the view beyond the windshield changing. "Everything is multiplying!"

Sliding into his seat, Derek looked from her to the parking lot outside the window. "What do you mean?"

"There is two of everything!" She looked at him. "There are even two of you!"

Smothering a grin, he put out a hand to catch her chin. "Close your eyes." She did. "Take a deep breath." He watched her comply. "How do you feel?"

"I cannot explain—like I am floating?"

"Do you feel sick? Is your stomach upset?"

She tried to shake her head in his hand.

He sighed. "You'll live."

Her eyes opened to meet his, and she was relieved to see there was only one of him once more. "That is good?"

His smile was wry. "Why didn't you tell me champagne would have this effect on you?"

A frown curved her mouth. "How could I know what it would do if I have never tried it before?"

"Don't they have liquor on Takyam?"

"Liquor?" It was hard to think.

"Alcohol. Intoxicating beverages. Something you drink to feel good—like a liquid drug."

Her frown deepened. "Harbisian ale is very popular, and Takyam has Sliskin. It makes my head feel quite light."

"Like champagne?" As she leaned back against her seat, her hair was glowing in the lamplight. She appeared soft, appealing, and as he watched, she turned to look at him.

"You wish to kiss me."

A smile spread slowly across his mouth as he sat with one arm draped over the back of her seat. "Reading my mind again?" He raised his other hand to caress the soft skin of her throat, trying to remind himself that she was an alien. "Can I kiss you?"

He was very close, and it was difficult to tell if it was he or the champagne making her head and blood swim. "I like it when you do."

"Do you?"

His lips came to hover over hers. Their breaths mingled, and when she would have opened her mouth to speak, his covered hers with silent warmth. She closed her eyes.

The beat of her heart as his hand skipped across her ribs to pull her close was strong and steady against his palm. That it came from her right side and not her left was something he didn't consciously notice. The only thing different about her that he was aware of was that, rather than melt against him, she seemed to merge into him. He didn't know where he ended and she began. He lifted his head to stare down into her eyes, pale blue orbs of light still clouded with the taste of champagne but alert enough to be darkened by passion. He stilled as her hand lifted to trace the line of his jaw.

"You have gold in your eyes."

The whispered words made him smile. "They're hazel, like my mother's."

She smiled, too. Under his gaze and beneath the touch of his hand that lay hot and strong against her ribs beneath her breast, she was flooded by a warmth she'd never before experienced. His thigh rested against hers, his fingers behind her head played with her hair, and his lips lowered to brush the tip of her nose with a butterfly's kiss.

"Yours are blue, like the sky around the sun on a clear day."

She sighed as his lips nuzzled, teased, and his tongue traced the outline of her mouth. Her limbs felt heavy, but her heart was light yet full—for him. His mouth closed over hers once more, and she reached up to circle her arms around his neck. He smelled good, felt good, and was like no other man she'd ever met. With him, she always felt safe. In his arms, she was secure, protected, cherished.

Kristiana's ready submission rocked him to the core. It was hard to let her go, to lift his head, to back away, and he wondered why. Was it a case of forbidden fruit? Did he want her because he couldn't have her? Because she was from another planet? Because she was unique? She had no guile. Her open simplicity, was what had attracted him. Her honest innocence. He'd wanted her before he'd known who—what—she was, or discovered where she was from.

Sagging back against her seat, she slipped partially out of his arms to gaze up at him. "You wish to mate with me."

"Is that wrong?"

"It is forbidden."

His jaw worked, and he caught her face between his hands. "Why?"

"Earth is not ready."

He wasn't. Not for her. But he wanted to be.

When his mouth covered hers again, it was a crushing embrace. Nearly brutal, almost violent, it spoke of needs and wants, and she trembled under his power. But she wasn't afraid. Not of him. Her fear was for herself and for what she would lose when she lost him. She tried to wrap herself around him, but suddenly he was pulling away.

"We have to get you something to eat." He caught her chin in his fingers, fighting the heat of his blood and the desire to possess. It wasn't a simple case of man wanting woman anymore. It was Earth male wanting alien female. "We need to offset the effect of that champagne."

His grin took her by surprise. It made her forget about the inevitability of future pain, about the doubts and worries and things that would soon come to pass. "A hamburger? I like those very much."

"America's favorite coming right up. Then," he said, starting the car and putting it in gear before taking her hand in his, "you can show me the stars."

And she did. From a hilltop far from the city, where the bright lights didn't interfere with the distant glow in the sky, she sat with him on the hood of the car and pointed out star systems light-years away. They munched on fast food, and he dreamed of places he'd never go.

"They all have four arms?"

Kristiana grinned at Derek's awed but appalled expression. "Yes, they are humanoid, like us, but they are all over seven feet tall and have four arms."

"Incredible."

"It is odd, sometimes, seeing other races, but it is difficult for me to be surprised. Takyam trades with so many peoples, their uniqueness in appearance is just part of the world I live in. The different traits of each humanoid or nonhumanoid race... Different skin colors..." She shrugged. "It is simply accepted that no two worlds will be exactly alike."

He sighed. "It's hard to imagine and yet, growing up with *Star Trek* and *Star Wars,* somehow it's not hard at all." He shook his head in wonder. "Other cultures, other civilizations, do exist. They've met and mixed, overcome their own problems and moved beyond their own planets."

"Earth will, too."

"When?"

She heard his hopelessness and took his hand. "It will not be easy. It was not for us. Before the common need to survive bound us together, we had wars and conflicts. But by being forced to work together, we were able to overcome many problems Earth is now facing."

His fingers linked with hers. "I guess we have to believe that. It's just that there's so much waste and destruction here. We keep pulling resources out of the planet and putting nothing back...."

"As did we."

He turned to find her smiling at him. "You almost make me believe in the future."

"You must."

His grin was eager, childlike. "I just wish I could see it. See the universe you already know." He turned back to gaze up at the stars. "It must be wonderful."

"I can show you."

Smothering another sigh, he looked again to her. "How? By taking me with you?"

She slid off the hood of the car and tugged on his hand still caught in hers. "No, here. Now."

Frowning, he followed her. "How?" he repeated.

She sank to her knees, and he followed, kneeling in the grass in front of her. "If you will open your mind to me, I will show you all the places that you wish to go."

"Can you..." He stopped when her hands came up to frame his face, and his breath caught as she knelt, shrouded in moonlight. He'd never seen anyone more lovely. She was more than an alien. She was a piece of heaven on earth.

"You must empty your head of all thought. Look into my eyes, and think only of me."

"That's easy." But as his hands reached for her, her pale blue gaze warned him to be serious, and he stilled as her fingers lowered to link with his. He watched her smile and suddenly he was flying.

Startled, he nearly jerked away, but the quiet in her eyes and the steady strength of her fingers linked with his held him safe as he found himself spiraling through space. Beyond Mars, Jupiter, Saturn, across the edge of the galaxy, he shot through a black void that was lit by stars and suns, planets and moons, the likes of which he'd never imagined.

A kaleidoscope of color burst through his mind as the Milky Way passed and he plummeted into a market-place where people of every sort gathered. Green-skinned humanoids, others with bright blue hair. Some had scales, others had flesh that appeared translucent. Scents mixed with the sights, but before he could attempt to identify any of them, he was whirling through space again to another planet and another culture.

Questions came and were answered with the blink of an eye. Canyons were crossed and rivers forged. He saw flowers of incredible size and color, animals of unbelievable proportion, and more people of unfamiliar features. A universe of the unknown. It was his to touch, to see, to taste, to smell. He felt as if he were there, among friendly strangers, on alien but habitable ground. And yet one place seemed almost familiar.

Following a stream down a hill, traveling a road edged with grass and wildflowers, he found a land that he felt sure he must have visited before, but the cities beyond the fields were spectacles of metal and crystal, blended in a harmony he was certain he'd never seen.

The buildings grew closer, gleaming in the sun, and he was swept along with myriad spacecraft scuttling and scurrying across highways in the sky. Below, people shopped and laughed, families gathered over dinner, and he left the air to enter a home where a feeling of love emanated from an elderly couple with pale blue eyes and pure white hair.

The smiles that greeted him were warm, but the vision wasn't something he could hold on to. It and the couple faded away, and he focused again on a pair of eyes much like those he had just seen in his mind.

"Your parents. Takyam." He smiled at Kristiana as the earth returned to surround him, and he again became aware of the hard ground beneath his knees. "That was your home."

Sinking back on her heels to watch him, she felt his joy enfold her as his mind remained, momentarily, linked with hers.

He laughed and looked from her to the sky and the distant stars above, and for the first time knew for certain that Earth was not alone. "That was..." His gaze came back to her. "Incredible." Reaching out, he gathered her against him. "Thank you."

Finding her cheek buried against the hard width of his chest, she wrapped her arms around him and let his strength surround her. "You are welcome."

But holding her close, he suddenly became aware of the chill of her skin, the stiffness in his legs and the cold feel of the ground. A glance at his watch told him that his tour through space had passed in more than a blink of the eye. It had taken hours. He tightened his arms protectively around her. "You're tired."

She didn't answer. She didn't need to. He scooped her up, and she abruptly found her face next to his. She smiled into his eyes. "See? You can read minds, too."

He pressed his lips to her forehead. "Only yours." And as her cheek settled against his shoulder once more, he tightened his hold and murmured, "Let's go home."

Chapter Eight

When Derek woke the next morning, his mind was spinning with visions and ideas and thoughts for a universe bigger than he'd ever imagined and for the woman who'd shown it to him.

Kristiana.

Rising to shave and shower, he remembered carrying her into the house and to her bed. The champagne and the events of the day had put her to sleep, but he hadn't been ready or able to rest. For a long time, he'd sat watching her in the dark of her room, overwhelmed with what she'd shown him but comforted by her presence. He hadn't wanted to leave her. Somehow she made him feel complete. He felt as if he'd been waiting for her his entire life. It was ridiculous to believe that was true. A fantasy, perhaps. Nevertheless, he was eager to see her again.

Yet when he went to look for her, she was gone. Her bed was empty. Panic sent him flying down the stairs, but the smell of burning bacon reassured him. When he reached the kitchen, he found her at the stove where she was cremating bacon and eggs in a panful of grease. Grinning, he joined her. "Can I help?"

Jumping in alarm, Kristiana nearly dumped the pan on the floor. "I am trying to make breakfast for you." But it didn't look like it did when he made it, and it smelled even worse. Her shoulders slumped, and tears filled her eyes. "I have ruined everything."

Reaching past her to shut off the gas, he took her by the shoulders. "Cooking isn't as easy as it looks. It takes time to learn."

"But I ruined last night, too!" she protested, raising a tearful gaze to him.

"Ruined..."

"Your dinner and your meeting with your friends. I made you look foolish." Her head dropped. "I am ashamed." He had wanted only to be kind to her, and on waking, she realized how disgracefully she had acted. Breakfast was to have been a way to ask forgiveness.

He caught her chin and forced her gaze back to his. "The hamburger was just as good as any fancy dinner, and the Pattersons aren't my friends."

"But they acted..."

"I've only met Beth once before, and Tom Patterson is a blowhard."

"A blow hard?" she asked. "Is that not something you do?"

Derek laughed. "No. Well, yes. But in this instance, it's something you can be. Tom Patterson is full of hot air."

Kristiana's frown deepened.

"He's impressed with his own importance and likes to talk a lot," Derek tried to clarify.

"Oh, I see. I know a trader who talks all the time. He makes everyone..." She searched for a word.

"Crazy?" Derek offered.

She shrugged, and her gaze dropped again. "It is what I think the champagne made me."

He grinned. "You did seem to like it."

"It was very... uninhibiting."

His grin widened. "Alcohol can loosen you up."

"I think I was too loose."

He studied the top of her head. "You didn't hurt anything."

"But the glasses and plates. I broke them...."

"That doesn't matter. But you do." He watched her eyes lift to his. "If I was upset, it was because I don't want any attention drawn to you. You're safe here. I don't want that to change."

"I'm sorry."

"There—a contraction. You're blending in better already."

She couldn't resist his smile. "We'll go to work now?"

"As soon as we have breakfast." He pointed to the stove and pan. "Let me show you how to make bacon and eggs first."

It was a simple task, something he'd done for years, but the pleasure of accomplishment it gave Kristiana to actually fry an egg made him feel as if he'd just helped a failing student pass a final exam, and her enthusiasm was infectious. Instead of settling for a simple meal, he soon had the cookbook out and was teaching her how to make French toast and pancakes. But it was the rich maple syrup that won her heart.

Licking a forkful of food oozing with the maple brew, she sighed. "This is better than anything I have ever tasted."

"Anything?" he asked, finding it hard to believe that something on Earth could surpass every other flavor in the universe.

She frowned as she considered. "Maybe not anything, but it is close."

He grinned and swallowed a forkful of his own, but a glance at the clock over the stove had him shoving his plate aside. "We're going to be late." He slipped off the kitchen stool and into his suit jacket. "Come on. As it is, traffic is going to be murder."

As his hand caught hers, she jerked back in alarm. "It is going to kill you?"

"Not literally, Kristiana. It's just an expression." He gave her hand a tug. "Anyway, we're not going to stay at the office all day. I just want to clear my desk so we can leave again."

Watching the smile spread across her mouth, he couldn't remember when the idea of playing hooky had provided such appeal. Of course, he'd have to think of a good excuse for Kristiana, a new employee, to be gone, but for himself, he hadn't left early, taken a vacation, or been out of the office unless he'd absolutely needed to in years. And he wanted to now.

Following him out into the garage, Kristiana hurried to the sedan's passenger door. "We are going somewhere special?"

His eyes met hers over the roof of the car. "Seeing as how you showed me the universe, I thought it only fair that I show you what I can of Earth." Her smile was instantaneous, and the emotion it carried made his stomach flip.

"You have already shown me very much," she assured him, liking the way his golden gaze surrounded her and thinking again of what a wonderful man he was—and of what a wonderful mate he would be.

Without looking away from the warmth directed at him, Derek shook his head. "Not enough. I want to show you more. As much as I can."

She recognized the sudden note of desperation, and her fingers tightened on the door. Could he possibly feel as she did? In such a short time... She couldn't imagine losing him, never seeing him again. She forced a smile. "Then we must hurry."

"YOU RAN a red light!"

"I did not see it," Kristiana protested as they reentered the house mere hours later to change clothes for their afternoon off.

"Don't they have traffic signals in outer space?" Derek taunted.

She narrowed a level glare on him. "We do not have such things as rush hours or what you call maniacs driving."

"Illinois drivers are supposed to be some of the best in the world."

"This I do not believe," she declared with a sniff.

He grinned and gave her a gentle shove toward the stairs. Letting her drive his car had been an experience. She'd complained there were too many levers to push and pull, but he'd been adamant that it was lazy to let a computer do all the work. "Get upstairs and get changed."

The smile she sent him over her shoulder nearly convinced him to go with her to help her pick something out, but he managed to go to his own bedroom instead, where he tossed off his suit to don jeans and a T-shirt before heading for the bathroom medicine cabinet. He wanted to check and dress her arm again before they left. As he started pulling items from the shelves, a sense of unease touched him.

Something was wrong.

Stopping, he let his gaze circle the room. Everything seemed as it should. He frowned, and his gaze hit the wastebasket. It was partially filled...but Kristiana's discarded shirtsleeve was missing. He stooped by the container. She couldn't possibly use it again, could she? But even as he pondered its absence, he realized the sleeve wasn't all that was gone. He didn't remember exactly how many cotton balls he'd used to clean her wound, but not a single one was left in the basket.

Standing, he tried to steady his heart as it jumped in alarm. It was only Tuesday. The cleaning woman he'd used for years didn't come until Thursday, and even if she had shown up on a different day, she wouldn't leave any trash containers only partially emptied. He looked at the open door, and terror hit him.

Kristiana gasped in surprise as Derek burst into her room, but he didn't look at her as she stood by the closet fastening a pair of jeans. He looked everywhere but at her before abruptly striding to her side. He spoke in a low voice. "Your backpack. Where is it?"

The urgency in his tone had her falling to her knees to pull her satchel from under the bed. But it wasn't there. Panic had her whirling toward him, but he held up a hand for silence and motioned her back to him.

"Is there anything in it you need?"

She shook her head as she returned to his side, and her fingers closed over the beacon she'd clipped to her belt. Fear was making her knees tremble.

He grabbed her shoulders. "There's a bag in the closet," he told her quietly. "Fill it with your clothes. We're leaving."

She didn't question him. She just did as she was told, coming down the stairs moments later to find him looking surreptitiously out the front window from behind the drawn curtains. Stopping, she froze where she stood until he silently held out a hand to her. The angry look in his eyes frightened her. She started to speak.

He immediately stopped her by shaking his head and calling in a loud voice, "Kristiana, I've got to run out for a few minutes. I'll be right back, and then we'll go."

Her eyes widened on his, but she didn't protest when he hurried her out to the garage.

"Get down on the floor, out of sight," he ordered as they climbed inside the car. "And stay there until I tell you to get up."

Squeezing herself into as small a ball as she could, she crouched on the floor and held on tightly to the small suitcase stuffed with some of the things he'd bought her. But her eyes stayed on him. He was her lifeline. He would keep her safe. Nothing would happen to her as long as she was with him.

Feeling her eyes on him, Derek backed out of the garage and onto the street. He purposely ignored the car parked by the curb a short distance down the road. It and the vague silhouettes of two men inside. But once he was driving away, he watched his rearview mirror and cursed himself for being so stupid.

When the government agents had come to his office, he'd been so cocky, so sure of himself, certain they couldn't possibly suspect him of anything. But what he'd thought had been a superficial investigation was obviously more thorough than he could have imagined. He was under surveillance, which meant Kristiana was, too.

With empty road behind him, he headed for the freeway, breaking every posted speed limit on the way. He couldn't know if anyone had been watching them at the restaurant the night before, but even hearing about it would have been enough to throw suspicion full-glare on Kristiana. Swearing under his breath as he merged into flowing traffic on the expressway, he glanced down and found her still watching him.

"Please, tell me what is happening," she whispered.

Putting out a hand to reassure her was instinctive. "They've found you." The fingers in his jerked. "But they're not going to get you. I won't let them."

The fierceness of his declaration soothed some of her immediate anxiety, but nothing he could do or say could alleviate the terror of being caught. "How do you know they have found me?"

"Your sleeve was missing from the bathroom wastebasket, along with the cotton balls I used to clean your wound. Your backpack's being gone just confirmed what I was afraid of, as did the car on the street."

"They are watching?"

"Not now. I don't think anyone is following us, but I was afraid they might have planted bugs—listening devices—in my house. I don't think it's very likely, but that's why I didn't want you to talk before we left."

She nodded understanding, even though Derek couldn't see her do so while he was watching the road. "What should I do now?"

"I'm going to take you away, to a safe place." He glanced down again. "Roham will be able to find you if you move?"

"I have a beacon." She held the blinking box up for him to see. It easily fit in the palm of her hand.

"Hang on to it, and don't be afraid."

Her smile trembled on her lips. "I will try not to be."

Derek kept hold of her hand until Carpenter Pharmaceuticals came into sight. He couldn't remember ever making the trip from home to office in less time. Once on official grounds, he didn't head for the main building or his parking spot. Instead, he made straight for the helicopter on the pad at the end of the lot. "You can get up now."

Kristiana slid onto the passenger seat as he stopped the car, and her eyes widened on the multibladed machine several feet away. "We are going to fly?"

"As fast as we can. Come on."

Kristiana followed him outside as two men came out of the small hangar nearby.

"Frank, Bob," Derek greeted the mechanic and pilot. "I need to borrow the bird. Anyone scheduled to use her today?"

"Not today," Frank said, shaking his head. "Want us to fly?"

Derek shook his head and grinned. "No, this isn't business, it's personal. Besides, I need to keep up my skills. It's been a while since I was out last."

"Well, she's all ready to go," Bob said, falling into step with Derek as he moved toward the helicopter. "Got a full tank. Know where you're going or how long you'll be?"

Derek accepted the keys and struggled to keep the smile on his face and the conversation light. But it was hard. "Not far. I've got to check with my passenger. Family emergency."

Bob nodded. "You know how to use the radio, boss."

Derek grinned and waved. "I shouldn't be gone for more than an hour or two." Bob backed off, and Derek helped Kristiana inside, fighting against the sudden need to pull her into his arms. "Strap yourself in. This ride isn't going to be as smooth as you're probably used to."

Just the takeoff was enough to have Kristiana's fingers curling around the handle of the bag she still held. The helicopter vibrated, the motor whined, and the blades beat over her head. She couldn't ever remember being in such a noisy vehicle before—except when her ship had been crashing. But, looking at Derek as he used the controls, she felt no fear for her life. He knew what he was doing.

"We have to confuse them," Derek said to her through the earphones he'd had her put on. "I'm going to take you to a special place they can't possibly know about. You'll have food and water, and you'll be safe until I can get back to you or until Roham comes— whichever happens first."

The breath caught in her chest. "You must leave me?"

Keeping his eyes on the instrument panel and away from hers, Derek clenched his teeth and nodded tersely. He was going to lose her. He'd just found her, but she couldn't stay. Not with him. Not even on Earth. He had to let—help—her go. "You're safer without me right now, Kristiana. But I won't leave you alone for long. After I drop you off, I'm going to head in the opposite direction and go to the airport. I'll tell the tower I've got a passenger who needs to catch a flight out." He frowned. "It'll be during a busy time, noon hour. No one will notice if I'm alone or not. With luck, we'll make the government believe you've disappeared, gone somewhere that you haven't."

"You will come back to me then?"

He shook his head. "Not right away. I'll have to go back to the office to return the helicopter, then back home for the night. I'll act as if everything's normal. If they don't stop me, I'll come to you tomorrow." He glanced at her. "You have to be ready to move again. But if Roham comes first, you don't wait. You get out." His gaze searched hers. "I want you safe."

Tears filled her eyes as he looked away. He was leaving her. Perhaps for good. She might never see him again. Her desire with him was almost enough to make her ask if she could remain. But if she didn't leave Earth, she wouldn't be allowed to choose her own destiny. Her wishes wouldn't be paramount to those who were chasing her. She was a threat, an unknown, and she would have to be controlled—or eliminated.

Flying over Illinois and seeing the intricate web of a civilization alien to her own would, under different circumstances, have brought fascination, but as the helicopter carried her toward an unknown destination, she felt only pain. The pain of losing a love just beginning to grow. She could find no joy in exploration and discovery. Not when she would have to watch him walk away.

Not breaking the dragging silence, Derek struggled with his own emotions as he thought of letting Kristiana go. But he couldn't keep her and he wouldn't risk losing her to the government laboratory that awaited her if she was caught by Ron Rogers and Tony Magrini. Yet, life without her. Going back to what had been, to his daily routine. Suddenly he could see nothing to look forward to. Just long hours, endless days, and lonely nights.

For years he'd felt he had a full life, a life with meaning. But he'd only been fooling himself. His life as it had been was superficial, without substance, without feeling. He'd been giving all his time, energy and passion to a company, an inanimate thing that couldn't care or share. True, Carpenter Pharmaceuticals accomplished many good things. Still, even it didn't give him the sense of the usefulness and satisfaction he'd been searching for his entire life. He needed people. He needed Kristiana.

The terrain grew familiar, but Derek couldn't bring himself to comment. Carefree chatter just wasn't possible, past recollections weren't important. Not when he was facing a future that would be impossibly empty without her.

He shut the engine off as soon as the chopper was down safely in a field. Through some trees, a building could be seen, and he hurried Kristiana toward it. "This belongs to a friend of mine. It's a summer cabin, but no one's here right now. It's spring, and it's the middle of the week. You'll be alone up here, and there's no way anyone can tie this place to me."

Kristiana stood back as Derek shoved his hand into an inconspicuous flowerpot and came up with a key to the cottage door. He threw it open and hustled her inside.

"Food might be a little scarce, but you'll have enough until I can get back... or until you leave."

She turned to him then, away from the strange room and the strange furniture to the warm strength of his gaze. Grief nearly closed her throat. "They will not hurt you for helping me?"

He smiled, wanting desperately to hold her against him. He shoved his hands into his pockets instead. "No. They can't prove anything. I'll just deny I knew the truth about you."

"But you will not forget?"

"Never."

Before she was aware of moving, she was hanging on to him, clinging even as he clung. His lips found hers, and she pressed closer.

Even though Derek wanted to keep her against him, he knew he had to go. He put her from him.

"I'll be back as soon as I can." He looked from the watery blue wonder of her eyes to the room around him. "If Roham comes before I do, if you go before I get back... I...I'll need to know you're safe. That you went with him and that the government didn't somehow find you."

She pulled the beacon device from her belt. "I will leave this on the table."

He touched it with fingers that weren't quite steady. "Maybe I can use it to find you again one day."

Her lips trembled, and she nodded. "I would like that."

The hands on her shoulders moved away. She was losing him. Tears slid free, but suddenly she was in his arms again and his mouth was crushing hers. Yet before she could respond, he let her go. Released, she stood, stunned and alone, as he strode out the door and out of her life.

The helicopter took to the air again with a roar.

Inside the noisy machine, Derek didn't see the trees and buildings and Illinois of Earth below him as he told an unseen radio tower of his approach into controlled airspace and of his intent to drop off a passenger and depart. Instead, in his mind's eye he saw stars and planets and species of people he'd never met. And he saw her. Kristiana and the dandelions. Kristiana and the dog. Kristiana with David, at the office. Kristiana in the kitchen, burning bacon. Kristiana flushed with champagne as crystal and china danced above her head.

Setting the chopper down a short time later on a busy landing pad at an airstrip where people were hurriedly coming and going, he easily blended into the crowd, only to return again after a few minutes to tell the tower that his passenger was gone and that he was returning to Carpenter Pharmaceuticals.

The chance of a lifetime. That's what he'd had. A close encounter of the third kind that no one but he was likely to experience. He knew he should be grateful, but it was sorrow that filled his being. At least until he saw his company's landing pad beneath him—and the government limousine parked beside it.

Cool anger took over then. It temporarily stripped him of the anguish of loss, soothed the conflicting emotions that were ripping him apart, and prepared him for battle.

When he stepped from the helicopter and onto the pad, he was ready for Ron Rogers. His surprised, executive smile was in place even as heated fury burned in his chest.

"Ron Rogers, wasn't it?" he greeted the government man as Bob reappeared to take the helicopter keys.

"Yes," Rogers agreed, accepting the warm hand clasp. He gestured to Tony Magrini, who stood in grim silence beside the government car. "We need to talk."

Chapter Nine

"So what can I do for you gentlemen? There's a question you didn't ask?" Derek asked moments later as he dropped into the chair behind his desk.

"Perhaps you'll tell us about the woman," Rogers said, pacing to an office window to look out at the parking lot beyond the pane.

"Woman?" Derek frowned.

"The one you just flew off with," Magrini clarified, standing beside rather than sitting in one of the chairs facing the desk.

"Kristiana?" Derek asked. "She's an employee. She had a family emergency, and I flew her down to Springfield. Why?"

"How long have you known her?" Magrini barked.

Derek's eyes narrowed. "Why?"

"It just seems surprising that the president of the company would shuttle an employee somewhere," Rogers soothed, his voice not edged with the hostility touching Magrini's.

Derek looked from one man to the other. "Excuse me for saying so, but the United States government doesn't need to know whom I do what for and why. If I choose to become personally acquainted with one of my employees, that's my business.''

"Unless it breaches national security."

Derek laughed at Magrini's stiff statement. "You'll excuse me, gentlemen, but you know where the door is, and I did plan to take the rest of the day off." He stood, but neither of them moved.

"When did you meet her, Mr. Carpenter?" Rogers asked, pointedly seating himself in one of the visitors' chairs in front of the desk.

Derek met his dark and steady stare for a silent moment. Ron Rogers was nobody's fool. But the man was out to hurt Kristiana, and Derek wasn't about to let that happen. "Let me guess. You think she's the alien you're after."

"You're not answering the question," Magrini pressed.

"Neither are you." Derek shrugged. "But, seeing as this is a national crisis, I met her a few days ago."

"The night you saw the crash?" Rogers suggested.

"As a matter of fact, yes," Derek agreed, retaking his seat with casual ease.

"You didn't tell us about her," Magrini objected. "You said you hadn't seen anyone else that night."

"I didn't make the connection with her," Derek responded with a careless motion of his shoulders.

"A hitchhiker?" Rogers asked.

"No. Well, yes, I suppose she was." Derek grinned. "She's a character, that one. You'd like her. Climbed into the back seat of my car when I wasn't looking. I didn't know she was there until I nearly hit that deer I told you about."

"And yet, even though we asked if you'd seen anyone else, you neglected to mention her to us," Rogers emphasized.

Derek sighed. "She's a woman, and you were talking about aliens. Kristiana was coming into Chicago with nowhere to go, no one to help her, and she needed a job. I liked her, so I gave her one." As Magrini's eyes narrowed on him, he added, "If she was this alien you're supposed to be looking for, in order to get from the crash site to my car, she would have needed wings. I wasn't at the station that long. Besides, she's as human as you and I."

"How would you know that?" Rogers asked.

Derek's gaze narrowed on him. "Maybe I should call my lawyer."

"Have something to hide?" Rogers countered.

"I don't like being grilled without a reason. You guys are way out of line."

"Did you check this girl's credentials before you hired her?" Magrini asked.

"Not my job, Magrini," Derek snapped. "Go down to the human resources department and read her application."

"Maybe we will," Rogers said, standing.

Derek motioned to the door. "That's the way out." But before either man could move, David Mallory was suddenly stepping in the room.

"Hey, I thought you were gone—" He stopped when he saw Rogers and Magrini. "For the day," he completed his sentence and nodded to the agents. "Sorry, I thought Derek was alone."

"They were just leaving, David," Derek said, rising and coming around his desk. "Ron Rogers and Tony

Magrini. They work for the government, and they're investigating Kristiana.''

"Kristiana!" David objected. "She's a special kind of lady. Why would they be investigating her?''

Derek could have kissed his friend for the unplanned backup to his own description. Instead, he smothered a smile. "That's what I was just telling them, but it seems they're bent on proving she's from outer space or something.''

David's mouth dropped open, and Magrini sputtered.

"I believe we discussed the importance of keeping our conversations confidential," Rogers interceded smoothly.

"This is David Mallory, my partner and CEO. What I know, he knows, and if you continue on this ridiculous crusade, I'll be telling more than David about your misadventures. I may not personally know my congressman, but I am very familiar with a few newspaper editors." He leveled a glittering stare on both men. "Now, if you're still interested, the human resources department is down the hall and to your right. But I think you should know that, before you get there, I'm going to call the director and tell her to make sure she treats all personnel records with the confidentiality the United States government insists on. I personally don't plan on being sued because of some bureaucratic screw-up.''

Magrini opened his mouth to speak.

"The door, gentlemen," Derek clarified, and waved to it.

Reluctantly Rogers and Magrini left, and David turned to watch Derek pace back to his desk. "What was that all about?''

Derek shook his head and dropped into his chair. He'd run a bluff. How much did Rogers and Magrini know, and how much were they guessing? Were a torn sleeve, some cotton balls and a backpack enough to condemn Kristiana? The items had been snatched earlier that very day. Could they have any results yet?

He met David's concerned stare. "You don't want to know."

"I think I do," David insisted. He jerked his thumb toward the door as he moved to stand in front of Derek's desk. "They weren't serious about this outer space stuff, were they?

Derek shook his head. "I don't want you involved in this."

"Damn it, Derek, if it involves the company..."

"It doesn't. It involves me."

"And Kristiana," David put in. "Where..."

"Gone. Leave of absence. I gave her some time off today to get herself situated in Chicago. She got a sudden call." Derek couldn't meet his friend's eyes as he spoke the lie. He had to reach for a pen and paper.

"She just moved here, didn't she?"

"She did, but she had to go home."

"Emergency?"

Derek nodded tersely and managed to meet David's gaze again.

"Must be serious for her to have to run off like that."

"Must be," Derek agreed, but the words seemed to clog his throat. It was on the tip of his tongue to confide in David. He was a loyal and trusted friend. But Kristiana was depending on his silence to keep her safe. He wouldn't risk exposing her, not even to David.

Shoving his hands into the pockets of his slacks, David studied Derek. He'd known him a long time—too long to be easily fooled or put off by half-truths. "I'm your friend as well as your partner, you know."

A smile broke across Derek's face at the less than subtle reminder. "A good one."

"But?"

"Trust me on this one, David. Please."

Dark eyes met hazel, and a slow nod came with reluctant acceptance. "I think I'll go talk to our human resources director."

Derek grinned. "You do that."

"Be around for a while today?"

Derek sighed as he looked at the mounds of paperwork on his desk. "Yeah. I think my day off is canceled." He reached for a file as his friend's hand settled on the doorknob. "And, David, if anything happens to me, the company's yours."

"Derek!" David protested from across the room. "You're scaring the hell out of me!"

Derek just grinned. "It's all on paper."

"I know that!" David snapped.

"Good. Now get out of here and let me get some work done."

Derek started to read and write, and he kept reading and writing long after David had left his office and everyone in the building had gone home. The compulsive work habit to the rescue again. He'd used it as a balm when his parents had died and Ann had gone. Hard work had always allowed him to close off any unwanted emotions, but it wasn't helping where Kristiana was concerned.

Weary and hungry, just before midnight he finally returned to the house he had lived in for years, but he found no comfort in the space that had been invaded by unseen intruders. Every sound and move he made, he wondered if someone were watching, listening, waiting for him to do something that would lead to Kristiana. Silently, he continued to worry about her.

The cabin should be safe. It couldn't be linked to him. It wasn't his. If the government was sure Kristiana was an alien, and if they were sure that he'd knowingly helped her, they would be looking for leads. He couldn't give them any. He had to go about his routine as if nothing had happened.

But something had. Kristiana had happened. She'd woken him up. Made him realize that the elusive something more he wanted out of life could be had. What he was searching for could be found.

Lying in bed, he wondered where her brother was. Had Roham found her? Would Roham take her away before he could get back to her? Derek wasn't sure which he preferred. To return to the cabin and find her there—and, thus, still in danger—or to find her gone, her beacon device on the table—evidence that she was safe. Either way, he was bound to lose her.

MORNING CAME all too soon and yet not soon enough. Derek was up and on the highway before rush hour was even close to starting. It wasn't his imagination that made him think he was being followed. He knew he was. Carefully. It made him that much more determined that his plan was going to succeed. As a boy he'd always liked to play hide-and-seek, and he'd seldom been found when he hadn't wanted to be. He just hoped he hadn't lost his touch.

The first order of business on reaching his desk was to write a long letter. It was something he seldom did, with a highly efficient secretary and myriad computers at his disposal, but this was a personal matter. A special task that needed to be seen to before anything else. He was a man who believed in being prepared for every contingency.

By eight o'clock, when Maggie arrived to start the business day, Derek had his letter written and was ready to hand his secretary the load of work he'd completed the evening before.

David popped in briefly, but only his eyes gave away his concern and curiosity. But he wasn't the person Derek was waiting for. He—or rather, they—didn't arrive until nearly noon. By government standards, Derek figured that time scale was appropriate. Bureaucracies seldom reacted with great speed.

When Rogers and Magrini walked through the door, past a scowling Maggie Kirkpatrick, who didn't like unannounced appointments or abrupt changes in schedule, Derek was buried in work and down to his shirtsleeves as he attacked the endless flow of paper. He sighed heavily when he saw the agents. "Back again?"

"We have a warrant," Rogers told him. "We want to see this Kristiana Cooke's personnel file."

Derek shrugged. "Fine. Maggie will show you the way to human resources if you can't find it."

The two men were back in Derek's office before he'd expected them, and he showed his surprise with a curious lift of his brow. "Problem?"

"There is no personnel record on Kristiana Cooke," Magrini seethed.

"What do you mean?" Derek asked in honest confusion. "Every employee has a record."

"She never filled out an application," Rogers explained through gritted teeth. "Seems they were too busy that morning."

Derek waved a hand at the agents and hit the intercom on his desk. He got the human resources director on the first ring. "Karen, it's Derek. What's this 'no record' business with Kristiana Cooke?"

"I'm sorry, Derek, but she never filled out an application," Karen's voice came back over the speaker. "It was Monday. We had that training seminar, and we'd just hired those two new techs."

"New techs?" Derek questioned, temporarily lost in the whirl of a rapidly growing business.

"You remember, from Trenton."

Derek groaned and reached for his calendar. "Am I supposed to meet with them?"

"Not until Friday."

"Thank God for small favors. About Kristiana..."

"As I explained to the gentlemen with a warrant, we'd planned to have her fill out the application later this week, but David told me late yesterday that she's on a leave of absence. He said you authorized it."

"Yes, I did. She had a family emergency. I don't know when she'll be back, and I guess that means we have no number to reach her."

Karen sighed. "You've got it."

Derek looked at Rogers and Magrini and shrugged in helpless eloquence. "I think we'd better talk about this later," he told his director.

"I already know what you're going to say."

Derek grinned. "I'm sure. Lunch Wednesday?"

"Thursday."

"See you then." Derek hit the button to terminate the conversation and made a note on his calendar. "I'm sorry, gentlemen, but I don't oversee every piece of action around this place, and mistakes do happen."

"Do you know anything about her?" Magrini demanded. "Where's she from?"

"Back east, I think." He shrugged again. "She didn't talk much about her family or where she was from. Frankly, I wondered if she was running away from someone. She seemed lost, afraid. I guess that's what made me want to help her. She needed a friend."

"You didn't think that was unusual? That she could be running away?" Rogers asked.

"You read the paper. Abusive parents, husbands, broken homes. I was giving her the benefit of the doubt," Derek countered, and swore he could hear Magrini gnash his teeth. "Look, I don't know what else I can tell you. My personnel people screwed up and I'm sorry, but I think you're barking up the wrong tree. Kristiana stayed in my own home, for Pete's sake. Don't you think I'd know if she was from another planet? Give me some credit."

Rogers stared at him for a long, silent moment. "All right, Mr. Carpenter. There's some other things we've got to check. We may be back."

Derek shrugged. "You're in charge. But, please remember I have a company to run." He went back to what he was doing but dropped his pen as soon as they were out the door. "Damn!"

Grabbing the briefcase he'd crammed full of clothing before leaving the house, he stood and opened his middle desk drawer. Things were heating up, and it was time to leave. What Rogers was no doubt going to check on were the results from any lab tests on the cotton balls, the sleeve and the contents of the backpack. Derek had no idea what those items would reveal, but he had to believe there'd be differences, at least in body chemistry if not in textiles. The only thing to be grateful for was the speed of the process, the steady plod of government as it worked out a problem.

Once obtained, the samples wouldn't have been processed anywhere locally. They would have been secretly sent via special courier to some secured laboratory, probably in another state, for examination. Once there, everything, including results, would have to go through proper channels before Rogers would get any further orders to move. That lapse of time allowed Derek a little room to think and plan. And when Rogers returned, Derek's plan was not to be around.

His fingers closed over the letter he'd written and sealed in an envelope. Staring at it, he took a deep breath and put it under the next day's page on the calendar on his desk. Maggie's last duty of every day was to turn the page over. When she found the envelope, she'd know what to do with it.

Swinging away from his desk, Derek moved toward a door most people took for a closet. In actuality, it was another exit, a back door, and he used it now to slip out of his office and the building in search of Frank, the mechanic. Frank maintained not only the helicopter but some company cars, as well. Derek had some errands to run before he met Kristiana. His first stop would be the bank. If Kristiana was still at the cabin, he'd need cash. They were going to have to run, and plastic left a trail too easily followed.

ALONE in the small summer home, Kristiana watched night fall with an onslaught of rain, and shivered. She'd been by herself for nearly twenty-four Earth hours, and each new sound, as well as some old ones, frightened her.

With Derek, she hadn't been afraid. Earth had been a place to explore and experience. But on her own, everything scared her. The strange animal sounds, the creaks and groans of the cabin, the unexplained scurryings that were, she hoped, more imagination than reality. And during it all, she kept thinking of him.

How long could Derek keep her safe? What would his government do to him for helping her? Not all officials were lenient on or understanding of those who interfered in matters of national importance, and she knew painfully little about Earth's justice system. The United States was a democracy, but what was perceived as abetting an alien invasion could make government security forces less than friendly to any citizen who got in the way.

Lightning flashed and thunder roared on its heels, shaking the cabin's rafters. Curling into a ball by the window, she continued to watch the road leading to the front door. Who would come first, Roham or Derek?

By herself in a strange world, she longed for the familiar, the security of family and friends and Takyam. Yet the woman in her wanted only the man with whom she had found such harmony.

It surprised her that she could love so totally and so easily. Roham had always accused her of having a soft heart and of being too ready to trust, but the link she'd forged with Derek had little to do with trust and more to do with affinity. To be sure, trust had initially forged the relationship, but mutual respect and understanding had secured and carried it forward into something deeper.

Smothering a sigh and ignoring the pangs of hunger grumbling in her stomach, she lifted the beacon clutched in her hand and wondered if it would ever bring Derek and her together again. Was it possible that the future would allow her to once more be with the man she would gladly choose as a life mate?

Bright lights cut the darkness outside the window again, but this time the glare wasn't followed by a roll of thunder. The beams came from the earth, not the sky. The breath caught in her throat. A car was heading toward the cabin. A strange car she didn't recognize as Derek's.

Panic had her sliding from her seat and into the dark interior of the house. She hadn't turned on any lights; she'd preferred the comfort of shadows. But the black corners offered little comfort as the car stopped and its lights were turned off. She clasped the beacon device tightly and edged toward the back of the cottage. Should she stay or run?

Swinging out of the car and into the rain, Derek swore at the torrent of water beating the ground and made a mad dash for the porch. He slid across it, grabbing the doorknob and shoving the door even before he stopped moving. Alarm pounded when he found it opened easily. Unlocked and dark, the cabin appeared deserted. Stepping inside, he feared the worst. "Kristiana?"

A squeal greeted him seconds before a warm body hit his and carried him to the floor. Laughing as kisses were pressed over his face, he finally managed to push his assailant away. "Does this mean you're glad to see me?"

Kristiana grinned at him as he pushed himself to a sitting position and lightning flared outside the door, illuminating his wet face. He tasted of rain and wind and earth and man. "You have come to stay with me?"

"I have come for you."

"I am glad."

In the flashing light from skies streaked by nature's electricity, he caught the back of her neck in one hand. "You're not using contractions."

"I do not care."

And neither did he. Not when the warmth of her lips found his again. He just gave in to her embrace, letting her push him to the floor to straddle him where he lay. When she sat back, he caught a fistful of golden-white hair. "I could get used to greetings like this, but I think we're smashing the french fries."

"French fries!"

He laughed as she attacked his coat, looking for the food he'd brought. "They may be cold."

She found one and hastily swallowed it. "They are still wonderful." She held one out for him, and they sat on the floor eating until the food was gone.

"I'm glad you're here," he told her as she curled up next to him. They were sitting by the open door, his back against the jamb and the rain that continued to pound the ground.

"Me, too."

"It's silly, I suppose. I know you have to leave, that I'll have to say goodbye, but—"

She covered his mouth with her fingers. "It will happen soon enough."

He took her hand in his. "We have to go." He sighed. "I think we're safe here, but I don't want to take the chance. The government agents were waiting for me at my office when I got back yesterday, and they returned today, looking for you. Unless your blood matches ours exactly, they'll keep coming back. They might even have shown up again after I left."

She frowned. "I do not think they will find a match. We have never—how would you say—sampled Earth blood. We know it is red like ours, and we know of your body structure. We are much the same on Takyam, but while our planets and people are very similar, I think there will be some differences."

"My thinking, too. So, on the chance Roham hadn't come yet, I snuck out the back door, took a company car to the bank, rented another car and went to another bank, rented a second car and went to a different bank, and got a third car before stopping at the bank again."

"Why did you go to the bank so often? And why did you need so many cars?"

"To get money. They can't track cash, but they can track rental cars." He sighed. "Once they realize what I've done, they'll know I'm with you. That means we should get out of this state as quickly as possible."

She stood with him. "Where will we go?"

He shrugged. "To Indiana for now. I'll call David tomorrow to find out what—if anything—is happening. After that, we'll decide how far we need to go. But wherever it is, it has to be someplace we can stay long enough for Roham to reach you."

Chapter Ten

"David?"

"Derek? Where the hell are you?"

"My questions first," Derek countered. "Where are you taking this call?" He was in a hotel room with Kristiana, the same Indianapolis hotel he'd stayed in the day before he'd met her. It was noon, and he felt refreshed. After driving until nearly midnight, he'd checked them in and they'd immediately fallen asleep. Now, having just taken Kristiana to the restaurant downstairs, he was ready to take her one step closer to her brother, but first he needed to know how badly the government wanted her.

David swore. "The conference room. I'd planned to have your call forwarded by my answering service to some neutral location, but I couldn't get out of the building."

Derek frowned. "It may not be safe to talk. Tell me quickly what's happening."

"Those two came back yesterday afternoon—Rogers and Magrini. You weren't in your office so Maggie asked me where you'd gone. Your car was still in the lot, so I figured you were around somewhere. They insisted we search, but obviously we never found you."

"They weren't happy," Derek offered.

"Hardly. Especially when we finally discovered that you'd taken a company car and disappeared." David swore again. "They're back today grilling everybody about you and Kristiana." He sighed. "Derek, about what you wrote. Is it true?"

"Cross my heart." His eyes found Kristiana's as she came to sit beside him on the bed. He'd told David about her in the letter he'd left on his desk the day before. He'd explained everything.

"Jeez," David murmured. "What are you going to do?"

"Get her someplace safe. I'm not letting them have her."

"Absolutely not" came the hearty agreement. "She's a human being, not a lab rat."

Derek grinned. "I knew there was a reason we're such good friends."

"What can I do?"

"Nothing. You've done it. I needed to know where they were and what they're doing."

David growled into the phone. "Driving me crazy is what they're doing."

"Just keep the company running."

"You're coming back?"

Derek heard the alarm in his friend's voice and looked again at Kristiana, who was quietly watching him. "I plan to."

"You don't sound too happy about it." The silence stretched across the telephone line. "You like her."

"Too much."

"She seemed special. I wish... I've got a million questions."

Derek grinned. "I don't have all the answers."

"None of us do." David paused and looked to the door. He thought he could hear someone calling his name. "Look, I've got to go. Be careful."

"I will."

"Oh, and one more thing. There's some guy here named Roham. Maggie hasn't been able to get rid of him. Do you know what he wants?"

"Roham?" Derek repeated, and sat up straighter on the bed. Beside him Kristiana's eyes widened, as he reached for her hand. "He's waiting there?"

"Yes, what should I tell him?"

Derek's mind raced to find an impromptu answer—one that wouldn't put Kristiana's brother in danger. In his rush to get Kristiana to safety, he hadn't thought about the possibility of her brother tracking her to where, until recently, she had been. "Damn, I forgot about him. Didn't even tell Maggie he was coming."

"Yeah, she's a little peeved."

Derek sighed and tried to sound casual as he attempted to provide a plausible, off-the-cuff story. "Listen, just tell him the truth. I forgot he was coming, extend my apologies, and give him a message. It's from his sister. I saw her a few days ago and she asked me to pass it on when I met with him today."

"Okay, shoot."

"Tell him I'll get together with him soon. But more important, let him know that his sister said she'll meet him where they met before when they stopped here for a visit."

"Where they met before?"

"He'll understand. Just tell him she'll meet him where they met before and to hurry or she might have to go away with someone else."

"Strange family."

"You'll never know." Derek laughed, squeezing Kristiana's hand. "Just tell him right away, and he'll get out of your hair. You've got enough to worry about right now."

"You, too."

"I'll be all right."

"How will I know that? What if they catch you and take you away to some government funny farm?"

"Such trust."

"Derek..."

"I'll get a message to you somehow."

"When?"

"As soon as I can. I'd better go." Derek hung up. "Roham's at the office."

"He must go! If they find him..."

Derek caught her arms. "David's telling him to leave. I just hope he understands that I want him to go to Wyoming." Derek shook his head. "Why did he go to the office?"

"He would have studied my movements before coming for me. He would have watched to see where I went and where I stayed, to determine when he could meet me." She bit her lip. "It would have been difficult for Roham to get so deeply into the city. He would have had to leave his ship outside the city limits and make his way to where he thought I would be." Her shoulders fell. It would have been very difficult to walk so far—it would have taken all night. "And then I was not there for him."

Derek slipped his arm around her. "It's not your fault, Kristiana. You couldn't have known this would happen." He hugged her tightly. "He'll understand." Derek sighed. "Let's just hope he knows where we want to go and what we want to do, and that the government doesn't catch on to what we're planning.''

As DAVID LEFT the conference room, he was unaware that a recording device a few miles away had just clicked off. Like Derek, he worried about the harm the government might unwittingly do in the interest of national security. He didn't have much confidence in bureaucratic mentalities or efficiency, but he didn't like to underestimate the powers that be, either. He just wanted Derek back, and safe—and the federal agents out of Carpenter Pharmaceuticals.

Moving past an arm-waving Maggie, David headed for the man named Roham. Assuming it was a last name, he put on a smile and stuck out his hand. "Mr. Roham, I finally heard from Derek," David said, pulling the big man to his feet and toward the door in one motion. But as he looked up into pale blue eyes, his heart suddenly skipped. "My God..."

Quickly David looked around for the government agents who seemed to be lingering everywhere—but none were near at the moment. He turned back to the tall, broad-shouldered man with golden-white hair who suddenly appeared all too familiar.

"You're looking for Kristiana, not Derek, aren't you?" he asked quietly.

Roham's eyes narrowed on the man with dark hair and eyes. "I am her brother."

David swallowed and motioned toward the door. "We have to get you out of here."

Ready to argue, determined not to leave without Kristiana, Roham started to resist. But the sense of urgency filling David touched him, and he allowed himself to be led away.

"Our government is searching for her. Here. Now," David said in a low voice as he tried to act as if he were merely escorting a visitor to the door. "Derek has hidden her. I don't know where she is, but she's safe, and he's trying to get her to you. He told me to tell you that she'd meet you where you met before when you stopped here for a visit. He also said to tell you to hurry or she might have to go away with someone else." David stopped at the glass doors leading to the sidewalk. "I didn't make the connection at the time, but he must mean the government agents would take her away if they catch up with her." He gestured helplessly. "I don't know any more. I'm sorry."

"I believe I understand," Roham assured him gravely, extending a hand in what he knew to be an Earthly gesture for greeting and parting. "You are a friend."

David accepted the hard hand with a steady grip. "I wish I could do more."

"You have done enough."

Watching Roham leave, David was filled with more emotions than he knew how to deal with. Wonder and awe at an unbelievable encounter, terror and fear for a friend in jeopardy, and hope that two kind people from a planet he didn't know would reach safety.

Taking a deep breath, David ran a hand through his hair and turned back toward his office. The government was waiting.

"THERE! That's perfect!"

Kristiana grabbed the dashboard as Derek shouted and brought the rental car to a sudden halt. They'd left the hotel and were on their way out of the city when, without warning, he had brought the vehicle to an abrupt stop at the curb. She followed his pointing finger to an automobile, labeled with a large sign, parked in a driveway. "The car that is for sale? You wish to buy it?"

Derek jumped out of the car, and she scrambled to follow him. "It'll be virtually untraceable, Kristiana. If we keep the rental car, eventually we could be caught. If we go to a dealer, we have to fill out papers. But if we buy something like this, from a guy on the street, all he'll be interested in is making the sale and getting his money."

She followed him as she circled the big blue automobile. To her, it did not seem in prime condition. Rust marred the surface, as did several dents. "It is old."

"I don't care if it's old, as long as it runs." Derek turned as the door to the house adjacent to the driveway opened and a man stepped outside to join them. Derek nodded in greeting. "Selling your car here?"

"My wife's actually," the balding but otherwise grayhaired man said. "With both of us retired now, we don't need two cars."

Derek circled it again. "Looks to be in pretty good condition."

"It's been well maintained, low mileage. The wife just used it to go to and from work."

Kristiana stood back, listening, observing, and staring in disbelief at the automobile in question. All of the cars Derek drove had been shiny and new, of higher quality by far than this one he was thinking of purchasing. It did not seem to be a very good deal to her. But then, some of the fastest spacecrafts she'd seen didn't look very fancy from the outside, either....

"Why don't you drive it around the block, kick the tires," the old man suggested. "Here's the keys. You and the missus try her out."

Kristiana moved to join Derek as he motioned her forward, thinking he wanted her assistance. "Do you want me to kick the tires?"

Derek suppressed a laugh and urged her inside. "It's an expression."

She frowned at him as he started the car. "You have many strange expressions." They rolled out onto the street. "What is the 'missus' he wished you to try out?"

"You."

Puzzled, she shook her head. "I am a 'missus'? I do not know that word."

Derek grinned. "It means 'wife.' He thinks you're my wife."

A smile abruptly lit her face. "Your mate?"

His stomach flipped as he braked at a stop sign and turned to find her watching him. Could the possibility please her as much as it unexpectedly did him? Since his split with Ann, he'd unconsciously avoided the possibility of such an entanglement. Now he knew that to live without love was not to live at all. But for Kristiana and him, the likelihood of any future was remote. Nevertheless, he reached out and caught her hand in his. "Let's concentrate on test-driving, shall we?"

But it was difficult for Kristiana, once the thought had been planted, to focus only on finding a way to get away from Derek when she only wanted to stay near him. Especially when she contemplated the idea of being his mate... Yet she had no choice. Earth provided her none—even if Derek wished her to be his. A frown pulled at her mouth. She thought he did, but he had not asked her to join with him. Her frown deepened. Perhaps it was the females of Earth who initiated the mating ritual....

"We're going to buy the car, and you're going to drive it to the airport," Derek said, interrupting her thoughts moments later as he pulled back into the driveway.

"We are going to fly again?"

"No, but we're going to try to make the feds think we did."

"I do not understand."

"We're going to take two separate cars to the airport. You're going to drive this one, and I'm going to drive the rental car. When we get to the parking lot at the terminal, I'll leave the rental car there for the government agents to find."

"And they will think we flew away when we will really be driving away in our new car."

"Exactly." He grinned at her quick grasp of the matter—and at the thought of Rogers and Magrini running around in circles. "We're going to make them spin their wheels a little."

"Spin their..." She met his stare. "An expression." He got out of the car, and she shook her head. When she got back to Takyam, she would have to explain to Roham and the council that they simply did not have a firm grasp of the Earth's English language.

THE DRIVE to the airport was one filled with terror. Even though she'd maneuvered through many a space port, Kristiana could not recall ever seeing so many vehicles zip past, around or in front of her at the same time—and none ever blew a horn. It was a trial she wasn't sure she'd survive. One man even raised a fist to wave a finger at her. It was a most peculiar gesture, and his irate expression made her believe it was not one of happy greeting.

"I do not think I like your Earth travel," she told Derek a short time later, gladly vacating the driver's seat as he climbed inside. He had left the rental car in the airport parking lot, and she was more than happy to let him get behind the wheel.

"Why not?" Derek asked as a jet screeched into takeoff overhead.

Wincing, she curled up next to him on the bench seat and wrapped both her arms around his right one as he put the car in gear and headed back to the freeway. "It is very noisy, very crowded, and very uncontrolled."

"There aren't any accidents in space? Your craft don't run into each other?"

"Radar makes it very rare."

He grinned. "On Earth the radar is in the squad cars, where police sit trying to catch speeders."

"Speeders?"

"People who break the posted speed limit," he explained, pointing first to a sign on the side of the road and then to the car's speedometer. "You do have speed standards in space, at least around planets?"

"Of course."

He grunted. "At least we have something in common."

She grinned and hugged his arm. She felt secure again with him beside her. "Tell me where we are going."

"St. Louis."

"A city?"

"Yes, in Missouri, which is in the middle of the United States."

She nodded. "It is named after a deity?"

"A deity?" He glanced at her, enjoying the feel of her warmth against him. Surprisingly, despite the danger, having her close relaxed him. "You mean because of the *saint?*"

"Saint Louis was an important person?"

"Actually, I don't know if he was a person at all." He smiled at her confusion. "The history—and sometimes the myths—behind ancient saint names and place names is often a long story. But if I remember correctly, this particular case has something to do with the French once owning part of the United States."

"I think I understand."

He wasn't sure she did. "We name sites after historical figures or events, don't you?"

"Yes."

"See? Something else in common."

She rested her head on his shoulder, inhaling his scent and trying to memorize it. When she left, she wanted to remember everything about him. "You would like Takyam. You would see we have much in common with your Earth."

"I like you."

A smile came quickly but faded almost immediately. "Do you think I am pretty? I am not too pale and ugly for a human?"

"Pale and ugly! What makes you say that?"

"On Earth it is as if you have a whole galaxy on one planet. You have people with many different skin shades. Hair is different and so are eyes."

Derek considered. He'd never particularly thought of Earth society as colorful, but to someone like Kristiana, from a world where everyone had the same hair and eyes, Earth might well appear to be a rainbow of people.

She sighed. "You are all mixed together. It makes me feel very plain."

"You're not plain. You're beautiful."

Her smile returned in a way that made his stomach muscles tighten.

"And, actually, with your coloring, you fit right in on Earth."

She frowned. "I do?"

"Next time you come, stop in at a California beach, where all women are blond and beautiful. The men, too."

"I think you are beautiful."

Uncomfortable heat burned his neck. "*Beautiful* is a word we usually use to describe women. Men are called *handsome*."

"Handsome," she repeated. "You are handsome?" When he didn't answer, "I think you must be."

"Thank you, I think."

She studied him as he drove, lifting a hand to brush the hair above his collar. "Why do you not have a mate? You are an important man. Most such men have mates."

"I almost took one once. Twice, actually." He sighed. "The first time was when I was in medical school. Valerie and I enrolled together fresh out of high school. We wanted to be doctors." He smiled and shook his head. "We were young. Full of ourselves and enthusiasm for all we were about to do. But when I dropped out to study making medicine rather than administering it, she didn't understand."

"But if she promised to be your mate..."

"Not all promises are kept." He glanced at her. "Isn't that true on Takyam?"

She considered and nodded thoughtfully. "You almost took another mate?"

"Years later," he agreed. "Her name was Ann. She and I seemed to have a lot in common and we thought we'd eventually marry, but as time went on, we realized we weren't right for each other. We broke up."

"You are sorry?"

He nodded. "I respected Ann. Liked her tremendously. But it's better that we're apart. In the end, had we married, we wouldn't have been happy."

"I am sorry." Kristiana chewed at her lip. "You will choose another mate now?"

"I could." He just hadn't thought much about it. Not until he'd met someone from another planet who was everything he wanted in a woman on Earth.

"You are looking?"

"It isn't always a matter of looking. Not here, anyway," he said, glancing down at her as she continued to watch him intently. "In America, at least, it's often just a matter of timing, of meeting the right person at the right moment, more or less by accident."

"And if you are attracted to each other, then you marry?"

"Sometimes. But sometimes the attraction is only physical."

"So you don't mate?"

He cleared his throat. Discussing the birds and bees was something he thought he'd do with his children. "Not exactly." Keeping his eyes firmly on the road, he shrugged. "When a man and woman meet and are attracted to each other, and have feelings of mutual appreciation, sometimes they will physically...mate, but they won't mate like you mean. Not for life."

Kristiana didn't say anything, and he hurried on.

"It gives both the man and the woman physical fulfillment and companionship until whatever stops them from deciding to spend their lives together causes them to drift apart."

Pleased with the explanation, he turned his head to smile at her and found her frowning. His stomach sank in anticipation, but she didn't speak. The silence stretched as Kristiana pondered, and he finally cleared his throat to start again.

"It's not accepted practice everywhere on Earth. In America, it pretty much is, though not by everybody, and it might not be accepted in, say, Africa or Asia. Every culture is different—just like every planet, I imagine."

She nodded. "Mating practices do vary from world to world."

He breathed a silent sigh of relief.

"Would you still like to mate with me?"

Chapter Eleven

Derek swerved to miss another car as the wheel jerked involuntarily under his grip.

"You said you liked me, but do you appreciate me?"

He struggled to find his voice. "I respect you very much."

"It is the same thing?"

"In this instance, yes."

"That is good."

He was afraid to ask why, and hoped the conversation was at an end. He suddenly felt ill prepared to be the teacher of Earthly ways, especially the most basic act of propagating the species.

"I like and appreciate you, too."

His pulse jumped, and the relaxing closeness he had found with her sitting next to him abruptly became too volatile for anything resembling comfort. "I'm glad."

If his response was cautious, she didn't seem to notice. Lapsing into silence, she appeared content just to sit beside him. And while he was relieved her questions had seemingly been answered, he silently longed for her mind-reading capabilities; he would have loved to know her uncensored reaction to his clumsy explanation of Earth's mating rituals.

Was it only general curiosity making her ask? Or was it a much more specific interest? The explosions of passion between them had seemed natural enough, and yet...

It was on the tip of his tongue to ask her about Tak-yamian lovemaking, but he couldn't get the words past his lips. Not when he was so close to the subject, and not when his stirrings of desire were doomed to be left unfulfilled. She was leaving. He would be remaining behind. Doubtless each of them, eventually, would find a mate on their own planet.

The idea had his fingers tightening on the steering wheel. It was as if he was sending her away to become someone else's! Jealousy brought a bitter taste to his mouth, but it was the way it had to be. They might like, appreciate and respect each other, but any other longings weren't meant to be satisfied.

He tried to focus on the long drive ahead—St. Louis was only one step toward the conclusion of their journey—but he kept finding himself wondering what it would be like when Kristiana was gone. She would leave, continue her life—and find a mate. But after meeting her, he somehow doubted that he'd ever find anyone who could make him forget how he'd felt when he was with her.

He didn't understand it. But suddenly it seemed as if all of his life he'd been waiting for her to arrive. Yet he certainly couldn't have planned on meeting a woman from outer space. Still, he couldn't deny the rightness of her presence, the sense that they belonged together. It wasn't logical, wasn't rational, but then, feelings often weren't. Nor were possibilities.

Glancing down at her, he frowned, then brought his attention back to the road. He was being fanciful, giving in to pure fantasy. No doubt the drama, the idea of forbidden fruit, was glamorizing and enhancing what he was feeling. The truth, far more likely, was simply that he was powerfully attracted to her. Pure and simple. Male to female. It was the only sensible explanation.

Unfortunately, he couldn't convince himself to believe his own reasoning.

ST. LOUIS at night was a city of lights and sounds. Habit had Derek heading downtown toward old haunts, familiar restaurants and hotels, but as he pulled the car to a halt in a parking space, he immediately pulled back out and left.

"Something is wrong?" Kristiana asked beside him, feeling stiff and tired and wondering how exhaustion could be making it difficult to keep her eyes open when she had done little more than sit in a car all day.

"I wasn't thinking," he said, once again on the street and following traffic toward the outskirts of the city. "We can't stay where I usually do. They'd look there first if somehow they figure out where we're going."

"They will know we want to reach Wyoming?"

Derek sighed and dragged a hand over his face. His eyes were tired, his back and legs cramped. It had been a long time since they'd stopped and stretched, and his mind was weary from thinking and reasoning and watching an endless ribbon of concrete. After the earlier conversation with Kristiana, bed wasn't something he could have believed he would find soothing—not with her in the same room—but he was ready to change his mind. "I've been trying to figure that possibility out."

She watched him in the light that flashed in and out of the car from neon signs and traffic signals.

"I tried to mislead the government agents. I told them that I thought you were from the east coast, but if they're questioning everyone at work, they're bound to find out you said you're from Wyoming."

"So they will think I would return there?"

"Well, they certainly know it's not where you're from."

He shook his head. "And lots of people, when asked where they're from, will give the name of a city, not just the state. Rogers and Magrini may find those inconsistencies significant, but I don't know. Maybe I'm being paranoid, but even if the government's slow, Ron Rogers isn't stupid. He could put two and two together."

"Two and two?"

"Like a puzzle," Derek fumbled to explain. "If you add two and two, you get four. If he realizes you mentioned Wyoming, and he knows it's not your home state . . ."

"I am a two and Wyoming is a two?"

"And your going there is four."

"I see."

Derek laughed and put an arm around her shoulders to give her a hug. "I never realized how many riddles we use when we talk. Let's just hope that whether Rogers figures it out or not won't much matter. Wyoming is a big state. He won't know exactly where we're going. Not that we do, either."

She grimaced. "I am trying to remember."

"I'll find you a map in the morning to help refresh your memory. Right now all I can think of is sleep."

And sleep is all Derek did, the moment his head hit a pillow a short time later, but when morning came and he was back behind the wheel, he found himself steering the car away from the highway instead of onto it. "Do you think Roham would mind if we're a bit late?"

Kristiana shook her head. "He will wait. But why would we be late?"

Derek grinned and pointed to the sign ahead. "Because we're making a detour—to the zoo."

He didn't know what made him do it. To delay was to jeopardize. But he believed the risk was minimal. Even if Rogers and Magrini did make the Wyoming connection, it would be impossible for the federal government to put an entire state on an all-out alert without giving a good explanation—and without starting a panic. Derek didn't think the government was ready or willing to do that. Besides, he wanted to show Kristiana as much of Earth as he could. After all, she'd shown him the universe.

Her reaction proved the undertaking worthwhile.

From polar bears to giraffes, exotic birds to reptiles, Kristiana observed them all with equal awe and appreciation, and Derek enjoyed listening to her gasps of delight or her happy comparisons. It was astonishing that so many species were similar to those she'd seen or heard of on other worlds or that actually lived on Takyam. Yet he supposed the possibility shouldn't be completely startling. Not when she and her people so closely resembled those on Earth and when similar humanoids were scattered throughout the universe.

"Ready for something to eat?" he asked as the sun climbed in the sky and morning passed into afternoon. It was a beautiful day, perfect for an outing, and during working hours, except for some ambitious mothers with toddlers, a daring grade-school teacher and her class, they had the walks much to themselves.

Kristiana sighed and moved away from the railing where she'd been watching a Bengal tiger stalk. "I love the cats. They are so graceful."

"And big."

She laughed. "They remind me of home."

"You have cats like this there?"

"Very much the same, and we have a zoo in my city like this." She took his arm. "But on one of the moons they have a zoo where the animals are not only from that world but from the entire galaxy. It is really quite . . ."

"Amazing."

"Yes." When she lifted her eyes to his, she felt her pulse skip. He was so handsome, and she liked the way his hand rested possessively at her waist as they walked side by side, hip to hip, arm in arm, as she had seen other couples doing. But he hadn't kissed her yet as she'd seen one man and woman doing. The unconscious yearning had her lips parting—and seemed to have him pulling her closer. Perhaps he was learning to read minds, too.

Derek had been trying to resist temptation. He, too, had seen the stray couples, and he, too, had been enjoying the feel of her body against his. To be with her, he kept telling himself, had to be enough. But it wasn't. Without thought, his footsteps slowed, he turned to face her, and his hands guided her into his arms.

Coming together was as natural as if they'd been doing it for years. Kristiana fit against him as if she'd been made solely for that purpose. Her lips blended with his in a union that transcended time. In his embrace, she felt complete. Without him, some part of her was missing. She pressed closer, but the eyes she'd closed in his possession were opened again—by a giggle.

It came from behind them, and Derek lifted his head to gaze first at her and then at the children huddled on a nearby bench watching them. When he looked back at her again, the smile on his lips nearly buckled her knees. He lifted a hand to gently stroke her face. "I think we'd better go get a hot dog."

"Hot dog?" she questioned, turning with him as his arm again brought her possessively to his side as they began walking. "They have dogs here, too?"

"A hot dog is food."

She stopped to stare at him in openmouthed horror. "You eat your dogs?"

Grinning, he pulled her back to him. "No, it's just what we call a certain kind of sausage. I don't know why. It's really made from pork or beef, and . . ."

And it was delicious. Seated beside Derek on a park bench, Kristiana stared at the hot dog in her hand. She wasn't sure she liked the yellow liquid he had squirted onto the oddly shaped piece of meat, but she did appreciate the unique taste of the red substance he had added. "I think this is very good."

"Better than maple syrup?" he asked, watching her lick her fingers, and swallowing the lump that formed in his throat.

"No, I think syrup is better."

"I'll have to get you some cotton candy to try."

She frowned. "Cotton candy?"

He rolled his eyes. "No, it's not made from cloth. It's that pink stuff on a stick over there."

But when they went to buy it, she saw something else she preferred. "Ice cream! They have ice cream!" She grabbed his arm as he pulled out his wallet. "I had it once before, and it was most wonderful."

Derek smiled at the vendor. "One cotton candy and one ice-cream bar."

Ecstatic, she danced away with him, stopping only when he held out a wad of pink fluff for her to eat. Her hesitation was brief, and as her eyes widened as the cotton candy melted in her mouth, Derek laughed.

"Like it?"

"It is like syrup!" Accepting more, she let the flavor roll on her tongue. "On Takyam we have sweets that taste much the same as those here, but I think Earth makes eating much more fun."

He grinned. "Eating is something you should enjoy."

She nodded ready agreement as another tuft of pink disappeared into her mouth.

"Here. You'd better have your ice cream before it melts." He tore off the wrapping and handed it to her, but she frowned on receiving it. "What's the matter?"

"It does not look the same as the ice cream I last had."

"Try it. I don't think you'll be disappointed." He watched her take a bite, enjoying the emotions racing across her face as the flavors collided in her mouth. He'd never thought such pleasure could come from seeing someone else eat. "Good?"

She nodded and stared at the bar on the stick. "What is this brown covering?"

"Chocolate."

"Chocolate," she repeated, the sound rolling off her tongue with reverent awe. "I think it is better than syrup."

"Most people would agree."

She held it out to him. "You must have some, too." But as she watched him bite into the bar, his gaze met hers and thoughts of food disappeared as a different kind of hunger warmed her insides. Unconsciously, she licked her lips. His mouth moved toward hers, and she leaned forward for him to taste her, too.

"You're lucky you can eat so many sweets and not get sick."

The words came as a jolt, reminding Derek that he wasn't alone with Kristiana. But the shock of intrusion was nothing compared to the alarm that made his heart slam against his chest when he turned to address the speaker. A sheriff's deputy. He fumbled for an answer as his gaze swiftly took in the uniform, the badge, the heavy gun on the hip, but he managed to focus on the smile on the man's face. "Not yet, anyway. We may regret it tonight."

The deputy laughed and walked on toward the vendor who'd sold them the food. As soon as he was past them, Derek grabbed Kristiana's arm and started pulling her down the walk.

"What is the matter?" she asked, hurrying to keep up with him.

"Bringing you here was stupid. Selfish." Derek swore under his breath. "I don't know what I was thinking of."

But he did know. He hadn't wanted only to show her more of Earth. He'd wanted to keep her to himself, to enjoy her for as long and in as many ways as he could.

Muttering darkly, he continued to rush her along, cursing himself for avoiding the truth. He was falling in love with her. For being a so-called smart man, he'd never felt more foolish—or more helpless.

The zoo gates and parking lot beckoned, and at the curb sat a squad car. Empty of its lone occupant as the deputy sheriff made his routine patrol through the grounds, the vehicle officiated as a visual deterrent to vandalism and rowdy behavior.

Derek started to hurry past, but something made him slow his pace as he went by the window. Pausing, he looked inside at a clipboard and pile of disorganized papers that had been tossed on the passenger seat, evidently awaiting review and sorting. On top of the pile there was a Wanted poster—with his picture on it. The breath caught in his throat as he leaned closer. Beside his photograph was a sketch of Kristiana. If the lawman had had a chance to look at those papers before going into the zoo grounds...

His jaw clenched, and he glared at the window. It was firmly rolled up, and the doors were locked. He couldn't retrieve the poster. He could only hope the deputy's memory didn't connect Kristiana and him with the pictures when he finally got around to organizing the papers. No one would expect, after all, that two people on the run would go to the zoo. But if the man did remember...

Hustling Kristiana across the parking lot and shoving her into their car, Derek hurried to the driver's door and got in. But as he put the key in the ignition, a quick glance at Kristiana made his heart stop. Tears were staining her cheeks, ice cream melted in one hand and cotton candy drooped in the other. The day of sun and fun had died. "Kristiana..."

She sat still in the seat as he dug napkins from his pocket and took the ice cream bar from her hand. His emotions were turbulent. She could feel them. They touched and mixed with hers, and she was helpless to stop more tears from falling. For a brief time, she had forgotten who he was and who she was. For a wonderful morning, she had existed for him and him alone.

The world had seemed a friendly place, but it had all been an illusion. Danger lingered near. As did the future—one that would carry her away from the Earth male she was beginning to bond with.

Derek caught her chin and dabbed at the moisture on her cheeks. "I'm sorry. I didn't mean..." But words weren't enough. He pulled her into his arms, and she sobbed against his chest. "This wasn't supposed to happen," he murmured, feeling angry and helpless. "*You* weren't supposed to happen." He'd been secure in his safe, sterile little world. But it wasn't what he wanted anymore. He wanted her.

Trembling, she clung to the hard width of his shoulders, taking comfort in the strength of his body around hers. But his words of rejection hurt. "You are sorry you met me."

"No!" He pushed her away a little to grab her by the arms. "No, absolutely not. I just wish... What I feel for you shouldn't—can't—be."

"We cannot be together."

It was a whisper. A truth that he realized hurt her as much as it did him. "No, we can't."

"I will never forget you."

He lifted a finger to catch her tears as they began to flow again. "Nor I you."

When he brought her to him again, the kiss was a promise of a future they couldn't know, and the tenderness of it ripped her heart. Resting her forehead against his, she took a shuddering breath. "You would make a very good mate. I think the Earth women must be...crazy not to have joined with you long ago."

"I think Takyamian men must be crazy, too, to let you run around on your own. If you were mine, I wouldn't let you out of my sight."

The declaration of possession made her tremble. "You sound like Roham."

"I think I'll like your brother." Derek reluctantly released her. "We'd better go find him."

"It will take long?"

"Days," Derek told her grimly, damning himself for time wasted in the zoo. But part of him couldn't regret it. Memories were precious things, and these would have to last him a lifetime. "We're at least five hours from Kansas City, and the only reason we can stay on the highway is that even if the trooper we saw recognizes us, he won't know what car we're in."

But it was the beginning of a race Derek suddenly realized he might not win. The government had posters out. He had no way of knowing how widespread they were. With no time to stop and search out newspapers or television broadcasts, he could rely only on the crackling of the radio to warn of any widespread alert. Fortunately, no late-breaking manhunt story was announced as he drove nearly nonstop to Kansas City before turning north for Omaha.

When evening came to cloak the car and their escape, though weary and wanting to stop, he pushed on. Traveling at night would give them a better chance to go undetected than traveling during the day, so he drove on as Kristiana sagged in the seat beside him. Omaha would put them only a state away from Wyoming, and getting her to safety was more important than any selfish need he felt to spend precious time with her.

Feeling ever more pressed for time, he decided to get off the freeway and skip Omaha, taking, instead, a side road to Lincoln. The old car was holding up well. The radiator was running cool, and the engine hummed under the steady pressure of passing miles. Unfortunately, along an empty stretch of country highway, one of the tires decided to give out.

The bang as the rubber blew scared Kristiana and had Derek fighting the wheel as the car started to shake. It was a fight he barely won as the blue Chevy shuddered to a halt on the side of the road.

"Derek . . ."

He put out a hand to squeeze her trembling fingers in reassurance. "It's all right. It's just a tire. There'll be a spare in the trunk."

Or, there should have been.

Kristiana stood in the dark, wincing as Derek stormed vividly at the empty air, shaking a tire iron at the sky. She tried to follow his heated declaration about the car not being any good without what he called "a spare," but for the most part his tirade was lost on her as he railed too much too rapidly. She was forced to wait for an explanation until he finally fell silent and sagged against the car in defeat.

"We are in trouble?" she asked.

Sighing, he turned to toss the tire iron into the trunk, where it vibrated in noisy defiance. "You are a master of understatement." He gestured around them. "We're out here in the middle of nowhere with no spare tire."

Looking around, she saw that, indeed, they did appear to be alone in the world. She shivered. The only lights came from their car and the stars in the sky. But possibly not. She touched his arm. "I think a light is on over there."

Derek swung to follow her gaze and frowned at a glowing speck some distance down the road. A building? Probably. But it was miles away. Still, it would have a phone. He turned back to her. "I'll go—"

"I will come, too."

Appreciating her anxiety at being deserted in the middle of a dark road on a strange planet, he held out his hand.

"You'll come, too."

Chapter Twelve

The building turned out to be a bar. A local haunt just a few miles down the road from a small town, Derek's hope of finding a garage and a new tire began to grow. He turned to Kristiana, tightening his hold on her hand as they stood in the parking lot, and nodded toward the door through which loud music and muffled voices could be heard. "We'll go inside and try to call for a tow truck."

Not speaking but staying firmly by his side as they entered, she wrinkled her nose at the assault of cigarette smoke, beer and booze. She'd been in shipping ports with such facilities and had liked none of them. They were always noisy, the occupants rowdy, and this one didn't appear to be any different.

If she'd spoken her thoughts out loud, Derek couldn't have agreed more. It was a rough, Friday night crowd that filled the place at two in the morning, and overly robust laughter echoed over the tinny sound of a battered jukebox in the corner. The room reeked of sweat and liquor, foul language bounced from one table to another, and in an obviously male domain, the few women present hung on to their men as if for protection, while taunting those who were alone.

Derek realized grimly that the bar was no place to bring a lady, and as some of the men at the bar turned to look their way, he felt the hair raise on the back of his neck. Yet he couldn't leave, until he got to use the phone. Giving her fingers a reassuring squeeze, his eyes met hers over his shoulder. "Stay with me."

She didn't need any encouragement. Clinging to his hand as he made his way to the bar and the bartender, she had no desire to lose the sense of security his presence offered. But the protection he could provide was limited. He couldn't save her from visual assault.

Her gaze collided with others at the bar as she passed. She watched their steady stares drop to examine her in a thorough head-to-toe examination when Derek stopped to speak to the bartender. Rough men in rough places were used to taking what they wanted. Roham had warned her of their kind, and she had seen them often enough—from a distance. She didn't like them close-up. They made her skin crawl.

Derek turned, and she gratefully met the reassuring warmth of his golden gaze. "The phone's in the hall. The bartender gave me the name of a garage to call."

Following his gesture toward the back of the room, she turned to take the lead as his hands settled on her shoulders to guide her through the haze of smoke and the maze of people and tables.

Faces blurred around her as she moved, a sea of unfamiliar strangers, until one in particular attracted her attention. Kristiana's footsteps faltered as a woman seated in a chair she was approaching pursed her lips and emitted a large pink bubble from her mouth. Starting small, the bubble grew until it was nearly as big as the woman's face. Kristiana stared in rapt horror as she drew closer to this new phenomenon, but when she reached the table and would have paused to examine the oddity, the pink mass abruptly broke with a loud snap and was sucked back between the woman's red lips.

Fascinated, Kristiana came to a halt. She wanted to see more. But Derek pushed her gently yet firmly on until they reached the dark corridor where a failing neon sign illuminated the word Telephone.

Standing aside as he grabbed a battered book hanging from a shelf, Kristiana turned to locate the woman who had made the bubble. Her eyes widened as the pink material again appeared from between the woman's lips. Kristiana held her breath. Steadily, another bubble began to grow, larger and larger, until, like the last, it broke with a crack and disappeared with a flick of a tongue back into the waiting mouth.

Captivated, Kristiana bit her lip and continued to stare in unabashed amazement as the woman's jaw moved in a steady rhythm. Perhaps the Earth female would make another inflating mass.

Kristiana wasn't disappointed. She did. It came as Derek began speaking into the phone receiver behind her. Kristiana gasped in delight and reached back to get his attention. But she froze when something else abruptly caught her eye. Someone, actually. Three someones. And they were all heading her way.

The men from the bar wore low-slung jeans, wrinkled shirts, and leering smiles as they approached. But their happy expressions didn't fool her. She backed into Derek as he hung up.

It took no more than a glance for him to realize that trouble was brewing. He was prepared to avoid it. If he could.

Stepping forward to put himself slightly in front of but still beside Kristiana, Derek slung his left arm carelessly around her shoulders and pulled her with him as he started to walk around the oncoming trio. But the men weren't about to let them go.

"We wanted to offer the lady a drink," one said, keeping his eyes on Kristiana and ignoring Derek. "She looks a mite tired and thirsty." The smile he wore grew as he nodded to her. "My name's Terry. This here is Hugh and Jim."

"Terry, Hugh, Jim," Derek acknowledged, looking to each man in turn. They were young, full of themselves, and each held a bottle of beer. "We appreciate the offer, but we're not staying." He tried to go around them, not loosening his grip on Kristiana.

"The lady might not agree," Terry objected, his smile somehow managing to look mean as he turned dark eyes on Derek and continued to block the way. "Let her speak."

"No, thank you," Kristiana quickly complied. She didn't like the men or the hostility that was suddenly rippling through the air. "We are leaving now."

Taken by surprise at her quick response, the three were unprepared when she slipped around Derek, grabbed his hand and pulled him toward the door.

Loath to turn his back on the three, Derek followed her anxious lead, not feeling secure until they were once again alone outside in the fresh, cool night air. "We can wait out here," he told her, tension leaving him on a silent sigh.

"We are not going back to the car now?" she protested, her eyes on the door behind them. She wanted nothing more than to get as far away as possible from the bar and the men inside.

"A truck is coming to pick us up. It will drive us back to get the car."

"But should we not—" The words died on her lips and she tugged on Derek's hand as the door swung open and Terry, Hugh and Jim stepped into the night. She didn't need telepathy to know their intentions were no good. "Please come."

Derek turned to follow her gaze, and his jaw clenched. Mean men in a mean mood, and he wasn't feeling much better. He was tired, hungry, and wanted nothing more than a bed to sleep in. But maybe a fight would be the perfect way to rid himself of some of the frustration burning in his chest, some of his helplessness about losing Kristian. He ignored her attempts to lead him away, stepping in front of her as the trio formed an abbreviated circle around them.

The man named Terry looped his fingers in his belt and smiled. "We'd like the lady to stay with us."

"She's not interested," Derek answered, feeling his blood begin to pump with adrenaline.

Terry grinned and looked from his friends back to Derek. "You know, you've got the bad habit of speaking for her. Maybe she'd like to spend the night with us instead of you."

"I don't think so," Derek said, silently reaching behind him to push Kristiana a short distance back. The odds weren't good—three to one—but he'd be dead before any of them touched her, and that meant he needed swinging room.

"I guess we're going to have to take her from you, then."

"You can try." Derek smiled and ducked as the first fist flew. It came from Hugh, the shortest, the heaviest, and the closest. Derek pivoted and moved in, slamming his knuckles into an exposed stomach.

Air rushed out of shocked lungs, but Derek was already spinning as Terry started to close in. Derek whipped his elbow back. It hit Terry in the face as Jim lunged for Kristiana. But she wasn't standing still. She dodged right.

Never having been in a fight before, she wasn't sure exactly what to do. But she had seen a few from afar, and she did know that remaining in one place was a sure way to get hit. Jim's fingers brushed her arm, but Derek caught hold of Jim before he could take another step.

Black fury drove the fist that lifted Jim off the ground. The impact would have been enough to stop most men. But, wiry and wily, Jim wasn't as soft as Hugh. He was a regular brawler. He swung in response and caught Derek on the chin.

Kristiana smothered a cry as she saw Derek's head snap back, but Hugh became a greater concern as he started to give chase. She whirled and ran.

Realizing Kristiana was in trouble, Derek gritted his teeth, blocked a blow, and threw a punch that made Jim see stars. Not waiting for the man to recover, Derek grabbed him and used him as a battering ram.

Hugh grunted as Jim hit him from behind, and he yelled as the momentum carried him toward the ground. Derek grinned as the two went down in a pile. But Terry was less than pleased when a flailing arm caught his foot. It made him stumble but didn't take him down. He managed to remain standing and kept sight of his target. Terry followed Kristiana as she struggled away from him and back to Derek, who was breathing hard but more than ready for another go.

Derek's grin widened, and Terry's lips thinned. At his feet, he could hear his friends groaning and cussing.

Losing wasn't something he was particularly good at. His nostrils flared and, sneering, he snapped his wrist. Cold metal gleamed in the night, and a smile replaced his sneer. He began to advance, and the two behind him regained their feet and quickly followed.

Watching the stealthy approach, Derek felt his skin grow cold. He had no weapons, only flesh to fight back with. Some type of retreat seemed in order. A frightened murmur came from behind him. Kristiana. His fists clenched, and his stance set. He wouldn't quit yet. But suddenly Kristiana startled him by dashing away.

She ran around the men, putting them between Derek and herself. He smiled. Divide and conquer. Apparently that strategy worked everywhere in the universe. And before the three could figure out what to do next, he stepped in.

Terry turned to meet a jab. It was hard enough to knock some teeth loose. He faltered to one knee.

Jim spun from watching Kristiana to meet Derek's charge. But Hugh's attention stayed on her. She ran again, and he went after her. And this time, he caught her arm.

Squealing, Kristiana whirled on him and used every limb in self-defense. Feet kicked, hands slapped, and nails reached for exposed skin. It did little good. He was three times her weight and size. Still, flesh wasn't as hard as teeth, and he yowled as her bite found his arm.

Lost in a battle of his own, Derek's neck snapped as Jim's fist found his jaw, but he still heard Kristiana's cry. He swung blindly and was rewarded with the sound and feel of bone meeting bone. But his victory was short-lived.

Terry recovered enough to stretch out a leg. Derek tripped, and Jim was ready. Quick and battle experienced, he jumped behind Derek to pin his arms.

Derek roared and humped his shoulders in an attempt to throw him off. But he froze when he unexpectedly found himself nose-to-blade with Terry's knife.

Trapped by Hugh in much the same manner as Jim held Derek, Kristiana watched Terry smile and wave the blade in front of Derek's face. She whimpered and strained against the grip holding her, but she was trapped.

Meeting the mad glitter of Terry's eyes over the gleaming metal, Derek braced for thrust or cut and cursed his lack of strength or cunning. It didn't matter that the odds weren't in his favor or that he hadn't been in a fight since eighth grade. His only thought was of Kristiana. She was depending on him. Preparing for one last, desperate move, he braced his legs for a whirling spring. He was heavier than Jim. If he could lift and twist . . .

Terry advanced, his smile growing. The knife came up, and Derek prepared to feel pain. But suddenly Terry was flying.

Stunned, Derek watched as Terry was lifted off his feet and tossed backward by an invisible force. It took all of three seconds for him to realize what had happened. It took Jim and Hugh more, and that was their failing. Before Terry hit the ground several feet away, Derek was ripping out of Jim's grip and sending him after his fallen friend. He took two steps toward Kristiana, and Hugh released her with a strangled sound that followed him as he raced for the back of the building and the shadows beyond.

Derek opened his arms to catch a sobbing Kristiana. His ribs hurt, his nose was bleeding, and he wasn't sure he'd ever move his jaw again, but he had her. He wrapped her against him as headlights cut the night, and Terry and Jim groaned in unison where they lay in a heap on the ground.

"It's okay," he told her as she cried and clung to him. "We're all right. Thanks to you."

She raised blurry eyes to him and gasped. "You are bleeding!"

He caught her trembling hand as she tried to touch his split lip. "I thought you said you weren't very good at telekinesis."

"I am not."

He laughed and hugged her as a tow truck rumbled into the lot and a man stuck his head out the open window to look at the two figures in the dirt. "Problem? I can call the sheriff on the CB."

Derek shook his head and, with his arm around Kristiana, moved toward the passenger door. "Forget it. We just want our car fixed."

"LET ME HELP."

Derek groaned as Kristiana rushed to help him pull his T-shirt off. The car was in the garage and would be ready when they left the small motel room to hit the road in a few hours. At the moment Derek couldn't see beyond the next minute, much less the next hour. Every muscle was beginning to throb, his face hurt so much he was afraid to blink, and his ribs, where hard knuckles had been deflected, were starting to ache. "It's all right," he protested against her anxious ministrations. "I just have to take my time."

Kristiana bit her lip as he slowly tossed the shirt aside. Blood was on his nose and lip. His cheekbone was starting to swell, and the way he was moving said he felt pain in more areas than showed visible injury. "I will get a cool cloth."

"Kristiana..." But she was gone. Sighing, he reached for a pillow on the bed, propped himself up against the headboard, and winced. Normally he would have insisted on their having two beds. It was what he had been doing so far. But he hadn't been in the mood to argue when the desk clerk had offered him a room for "you and your wife," and he was in no condition to do anything about the close accommodations. If worse came to worst, he'd take a cold shower.

Kristiana hurried back to sit beside him on the lumpy mattress, and he didn't try to stop her from dabbing gently at the blood or cuts. If it hurt as much as it helped, it was making her feel better, and he was too weary to resist.

"We should have ice," she said, and stood. "I will go get some."

He caught her hand. "No, no, it's all right. I just want to lie here for a minute, then take a shower and go to bed."

She sank back down beside him, feeling useless and ineffective as he took the dampened washcloth from her hand to hold it to his lip. He looked so miserable. "I am sorry to be so much trouble."

He tried to grin but winced instead. "It wasn't your fault."

She watched him look at the stained cloth. "You were wonderful."

He grunted. "You made me look good."

"No, it was you." She took the cloth from him to wipe his forehead. "I knew what you were planning to do. You would have risked your life to save me."

He watched as her eyes dropped to the cloth to her lap, realizing that in the stress of the moment, she must have read his mind.

"I was so frightened." She shook her head. "I have never done anything like that before."

The whispered admission had him reaching out to catch her face in his hand. "I thought *you* were wonderful."

Her smile trembled. "He is the biggest thing I have ever moved."

"Roham would be very proud, and I'm very grateful," Derek assured her, and watched the smile on her lips strengthen. He brushed her hair over her shoulder. "We make a good team."

But suddenly her eyes darkened under his gaze, the friendly glow between them started to heat, and of their own volition, his hands began pulling her toward him. He tried to let go when he found his lips hovering over hers. What he wanted couldn't be. But his feeble resistance was easily pushed aside. She brought her mouth to his.

The initial contact was startling. It made her pulse leap, but it didn't stop her from leaning forward to let the warmth of his body surround her. She ran her hands over his bared chest. The muscles were strong and hard beneath the skin, the hair covering it deceptively soft. She pressed closer, and he absorbed her with a sigh.

The silken length of her hair whispered across his shoulders. The cool touch of her fingers on his hot flesh soothed and aroused in the same stroke. And the sweet scent that was uniquely hers filled his senses. He was drowning in her, but he didn't want to be saved. Instead he let the whirlpool take him as, lifting her head, she pressed a kiss to first one of his eyes, then the other, before letting him look up to focus on her.

Her smile held wonders and mysteries that were ageless, shared by men and women throughout eternity but unique to everyone, and he wanted to learn her secrets. Until she spoke and broke the spell.

"I wish to mate with you."

Reality hit him with a crash. Derek struggled to a sitting position and tried to push her away. "No!"

Pain filled her pale blue eyes. "You do not like and respect me enough?"

"No," he objected, unable to make his fingers let her go, and forcing her to meet his gaze when she would have looked away. "I mean, it's not that. It's just..." He brushed her cheek. "You're not the kind of woman a man loves and leaves."

She frowned. "I do not understand. You said if an Earth American male likes and respects a female, he would mate with her even if he knew eventually they must part."

Trapped by her interpretation of his explanation, Derek was at a loss for words.

"It is my wish to be your mate."

Before he could protest, she was on her feet, stripping off her clothes in flowing gestures that left her standing in front of him in a naked vision of white and gold.

"I am yours."

The declaration had him sliding off the bed, all pain forgotten. The ache in his ribs, the throb in his muscles, the bruises on his face were lost in the mists of a passion he was trying to ignore. He reached for her. He had to tell her, explain about one-night stands, and commitments, and remind her that they had no future, but somehow only the present seemed to matter when the smooth skin of her arms came under the palms of his hands. "Kristiana." Her name was all he could say as she melted into his arms.

It was like coming home, to feel his strength envelop her. With him was where she belonged. Pressing herself to him, she felt the softness of her flesh meld with the hardness of his. A perfect match, a perfect fit, their bodies fused from head to toe. She sighed and closed her eyes as his lips met hers and new sensations overwhelmed them both.

It became impossible to think or reason. Yesterday, today, tomorrow—all blended into one and time ceased to matter. Lost in the warmth of her embrace, he could only surrender to a desire too long buried. His clothes followed hers to the floor.

They moved as if one. Hands touched, fingers caressed, and flesh began to burn. Quiet at first, the flames sizzled with exploration, but passion's coals were stoked. The fire rapidly grew hotter. They moved from standing on the floor to kneeling on the bed.

The mattress groaned under their weight, but they didn't notice. Their attention belonged to each other. Lips met and searched, and hands traced ridges of muscle or the softness of an inner thigh. Breathing and heartbeats accelerated, and the blaze erupted into an inferno.

Strokes scalded, touches tormented, and blood began to boil. The bed groaned again as he laid her down to wage a new assault, but she wasn't a passive victim. The heat was overtaking her, too, and as it rose to consume them both, she encouraged him with caresses that both aroused and guided until they joined in a fiery union that was nothing short of volcanic.

It obliterated the senses, rocked them to the core, and flowed with molten energy until the explosion's echoes died and they were left in the shimmering ashes of love's aftermath.

Rolling over, he carried her with him to lie with his legs entwined with hers. Above the bed the ceiling paint was cracked and peeling, but he didn't see it, or the dingy drapes, or battered furniture. He saw only her as he looked into blue eyes as pale and beautiful as the sky at dawn. "You are incredible."

She smiled and reached out to touch his jaw. She couldn't feel enough of him. Her fingers clung to the warmth of his skin. "That is good?"

He laughed, and the rumble reverberated in her ear as her head rested on his chest. "Yes, very."

"You are not sorry we mated?"

His smile faded, and he turned so they lay on their sides, facing each other. "Are you?"

Her smile was wondrous. "I am yours."

"Mine," he agreed, and pulled her close to cover her lips with his in a searing kiss.

The embrace held none of the gentleness she had just experienced, but the change brought no fear. Only exhilaration. Released once more, she stared into brown eyes that were speckled with lights of gold. "You still wish to take a shower?"

His grin made goose bumps rise on her skin. "Only if you come with me."

Regretting the need to be parted from him and ready to find an excuse not to be, she frowned doubtfully. "It is a small shower."

"We'll fit," he assured her, abruptly sliding out of bed to pull her to her feet. "Besides, it's another Earth tradition I simply have to show you."

Chapter Thirteen

"We must go?"

The regret in Kristiana's question matched that in his eyes as Derek met her gaze in the foggy mirror over the bathroom sink. "It's nearly noon. We'd better go, or people are going to wonder what we're doing in here."

She frowned and wrapped her arms around him, resting her cheek against the bare skin of his back. His flesh was smooth, but the muscles beneath were strong. She'd felt his power and gladly been consumed by it. "How will they know if we do not tell them?"

He smiled as he turned to face her, not moving out of her embrace. "Trust me. They'll know." He bent to find her lips with his, eager again for her taste and touch. But the kiss unexpectedly stung.

She watched him pull back to put a hand to his swollen lip. "It hurts?"

Derek sighed. "It's been a long time since I've had a fat lip." Or a black eye. But he had them both, along with sore knuckles and bruised ribs. He touched his tender jaw. "Maybe I won't shave today."

She wrinkled her nose at the shadow of whiskers that were slightly darker than the blond hair on his scalp.

"On Takyam, few have beards. Most men have their facial hair removed when they reach manhood."

Continuing to run a hand along his jaw, Derek considered. "I think I could get used to that."

She grinned. "Come, you must finish dressing so we can go eat."

"Hungry again?"

His smile told her that he yearned for more than food, and she wasn't ready to deny him. Back in his arms, she wrapped herself around him and clung. Too short a time is what they had. She wanted to absorb him, take him with her when she left. But he wasn't a flower to be transplanted. He was a man with a life of his own on his own world. She pulled him closer and tried to remember the promise she'd made to herself.

She wouldn't regret joining with him. She wouldn't allow the lack of a future to interfere with the happiness she felt in the present with him—even if that happiness would be fleeting.

She closed her eyes as the embrace deepened. Her love for him was something she had not expected nor been prepared for. Still, arriving on Earth without warning, she had taken him, too, by surprise. And deciding to mate with him once she realized Earth custom did not forbid it was something she had done knowing their relationship would and could not last. Yet her promise was hard to honor. Already she missed him, and he seemed to sense her fear.

He ended the kiss but continued to hold her close, hugging her to him. "I wish we could stay." For a day, for a week, for a year. Forever. He pressed his lips to the top of her head. Words lay between them unspoken, and he couldn't bring himself to say them. Not yet. The end would come when it did. They both knew and had to accept it. "Let's go get the car."

In moments they were leaving the motel, walking into the Nebraska sunshine with their fingers linked, seeing, in the light of day, that the small town they had stumbled on was bigger than they'd expected.

"Mornin'," the mechanic greeted them as they stepped into the garage. The place reeked of gas and oil and rubber, but his smile was warm as he wiped dirty hands on an equally dirty rag. "Your new tire's on, and I've a spare if you want it."

Derek grinned. "After last night, we'll take as many spares as you've got."

The man with the name Hank sewn on his overalls laughed and led them toward the big blue Chevy parked outside the garage door. "By the way, you should know that the deputy sheriff wants to talk to you."

The smile left Derek's face. He felt suddenly cold even with the sun beating on him. His fingers tightened around Kristiana's, whose steps had faltered as she'd walked beside him. "Don't tell me I'm going to get a ticket for having a flat?"

Hank stopped beside the Chevy and shook his head. "No, it's about the tussle outside the bar." He grinned. "Seems Terry Katz is claiming you threw him a good ten feet without even touching him."

Derek felt Kristiana's hand jump in his, but managed a laugh. "Really?"

Hank shook his head as he pointed to the new tire on the back wheel. "Just a formality when they get a complaint, you know," he said. "I wouldn't worry about it. Terry is well-known in these parts for drinking too much." He took the keys from his pocket and opened the trunk to display a spare, locked in place inside. "Figured you'd want the spare so I already put it in."

"How much do I owe you?"

Hank quoted a surprisingly reasonable sum for emergency service and gestured down the road. "If you folks are planning on getting some breakfast in town before moving on, you can find the deputy in his office two stop signs up ahead."

"Thanks, we'll do that," Derek told him, handing over the cash. "We appreciate your help."

"Don't mention it."

Kristiana slipped away to climb into the passenger seat, keeping her silence until Derek had the car started and was pulling out onto the road. "We will see the deputy?"

"No," he told her, his jaw tightening as he remembered the Wanted poster the St. Louis deputy sheriff had had in his car. "We're going to drive right on by." He glanced over to meet her anxious gaze. "Think you can wait awhile for something to eat?"

She nodded ready agreement. "I will wait."

And she did. All the way to Lincoln.

Poring over the map he'd picked up at a gas station the day before to help him plan their route to Wyoming, Derek sat across from Kristiana in a restaurant right off the freeway. He wasn't particularly hungry, even though it had been at least half a day since he'd eaten. "I think we're going to have to head north."

Kristiana leaned forward to look at the zigzag of highways on the map he'd laid out on the table to show her.

"I'd been planning on going straight through Nebraska, but if this last deputy has the same poster the one in St. Louis did, and if he makes the connection to us based on the descriptions those at the bar and Hank give him, he'll put out a bulletin about what kind of car we're driving.''

''And they will watch for us?''

He nodded grimly. ''I think we need to backtrack. Go east to Omaha and then north to Sioux City. From there we can cut across South Dakota and make straight for Wyoming, and Roham.''

''We must hurry.''

It was a statement, not a question, and each word was weighted with unspoken regret and sorrow. His eyes found hers, and his fingers wrapped around her hand where it lay on the table. He swallowed the ache, the need to curse fate, and the urge to swear at the ticking clock. ''We must hurry,'' he agreed.

THE RIDE to Omaha was silent. They both sat quietly with their thoughts of parting and feelings of sorrow, but they stayed linked by touch. Their hands remained locked together, or her palm rested on his thigh while his arm lay across her shoulders and held her to him. She couldn't decide if she was more afraid of capture or of losing him, and he tried to imagine what his life would be like when she was gone. Neither could find any happy answers, and both were prevented from trying when the sudden blare of a siren and the flashing of lights appeared in the rearview mirror.

''The police,'' Derek warned.

Kristiana's heart jumped as he pulled over to the side of the highway. ''They have found us?'' Fear had her blood pumping and her palms sweating, and instinct had her preparing to run.

He released the steering wheel to grab her hand. ''I won't let them take you.'' But even as he declared his

intent, he struggled with how he could prevent exactly
that from happening. Behind him, the officer was leaving his vehicle, cautiously approaching theirs. What to
do? Derek considered throwing the door into the deputy's midsection and speeding away, but the officer was
now alongside the car. He was ready for trouble. Derek
squeezed Kristiana's fingers. "If something happens,
you get out and run. I'll keep him occupied until you
can get away."

"But..."

He shook his head. There was no time to argue. He
rolled down the window to greet the man in uniform
who stopped just short of the driver's door. "Problem, Officer? I didn't think I was speeding."

"May I see your driver's license please?"

Evasion rather than response. That wasn't a good
sign. The poster and the fistfight. Two plus two equals
four. Derek's eyes met Kristiana's.

Reluctantly she released his hand to allow him to
reach for the wallet in his pocket. He was helpless, and
she was scared. Her gaze strayed to the rear window and
the squad car sitting with its lights still flashing. It was
waiting to carry her away.

Fear had her turning back to Derek, but it was the
deputy she found watching her instead. Bending to stare
through the driver's door window at her, his eyes were
hidden behind mirrored sunglasses, but his thoughts
were clear. He was after her.

Her heart leapt in alarm, and she quickly looked
away and out the back window again. She began to
concentrate.

"Hey!"

The unexpected shout made Derek jump as he pulled
his license from his wallet, and he turned just in time to

see the deputy leap away from the door and back toward the squad car. "What..."

"Go!" Kristiana shouted.

Derek was given no time to understand what was happening. Invisible pressure hit his right foot as it rested on the gas pedal. The engine roared in response as the car sat immobile in Park, and he instinctively grabbed the steering wheel as his gaze flew to the rearview mirror. His jaw dropped open when he saw the squad car rolling backward down the highway, but he grinned when he spotted the deputy running after it. He threw the Chevy into drive, and the car shot out onto the freeway to join the other traffic heading for downtown Omaha.

"You did it again!" he declared with a laugh, the mirror showing the deputy still running and the squad car still rolling.

"Fear is a powerful motivator."

His smile died, and he turned to meet terrified blue eyes.

"He knew who we were." The statement was cold, but the fear behind it was hot.

Derek's teeth clenched. The government was pushing hard. His fingers found hers trembling. "He won't catch us again." Pulling her up against him, Derek kept the gas pedal down as he raced into the city and onto the main streets. A parking garage waited ahead, and he swerved into it with squealing tires.

Kristiana held on to the ticket Derek handed her as the gate opened, and braced herself against him as he threw the Chevy around curve after curve until a dark corner and an empty parking space loomed ahead. She grabbed her pack from the back seat as he brought the car to a stop. "Where do we go now?"

"Out of here."

She slid with him onto the concrete flooring and studied the sea of automobiles around them. "We will find another car to drive?"

"Not here." But even as he took her hand, thinking of the bus station he'd seen a block away, he stopped. Next to them sat a car with the keys in the ignition. A Pontiac Firebird. It was a little flashier than he would have preferred, but under the circumstances, beggars couldn't be choosers. "Then again..."

Remaining by the Chevy as Derek went to the driver's door of a slick white sports car, Kristiana watched him try the door and, when it didn't open, put his hand through the partially open window in an attempt to reach the lock. Hearing him swear when the lever remained beyond the tips of his fingers, she quickly moved to join him. "Can I help?"

He gestured to the window. "By all means."

Smaller boned, she had no trouble getting her arm in far enough to grasp the lock and pull it up. "This is what you wish?" she asked, pulling back her arm and opening the door.

"It is what we need." He gave her a gentle push around the back of the car. "Get in."

She climbed in the passenger side as he started the motor humming. "We will buy this car, too?"

"No, we're going to borrow it." Noting the gas tank was full and the engine purred smoothly, Derek swallowed any feelings of guilt at the theft. Stealing wasn't something he condoned, but desperate times called for desperate measures. Right now he had to save Kristiana. Later, he'd find a way to reimburse the owner. He put the car into reverse and shot out of the garage and into the afternoon sunshine.

Kristiana flinched under the bright glare, certain someone must be watching them, but no pursuit materialized. They blended in with the other vehicles moving out of the city, and she reached for the map Derek had tossed onto the dashboard. "We will go to Sioux City?"

"And from there to Sioux Falls. The highway runs straight across South Dakota to Wyoming. It'll be a good eight-hour drive, but we'll make it." He glanced at her as she began to study the map he'd brought from the Chevy. "You just have to tell me where to go once we get there."

She frowned as she followed the highway west, seeking the cities he named and the state they sought, and just beyond the state's boundary she recognized a word. "Sheridan."

"It's in Wyoming."

"It is where we must go."

His stomach sank, and his foot eased off the gas pedal. Having a final destination somehow made him want to slow down, but, remembering the deputy, he pressed the pedal again. "You're sure?"

"I remember. It is what Roham calls a small city, and it is isolated."

"Lots of Wyoming is isolated. The Rocky Mountains cut right through the state, and they take up a lot of room."

Her hands tightened on the map. Roham was waiting, and she was suddenly eager to see him, to be gone and safe. Until she looked at the man sitting across from her. This vehicle had bucket seats and the gap separating driver from passenger, him from her, seemed to emphasize the distance that would soon separate them forever. "We will be there in one day?"

The tremor in her voice made him turn to her again. Tears glittered in her eyes. He swallowed and blindly found her hand. It was warm and soft, and he held it tightly. "We should be there tomorrow."

Without thought, she abruptly threw herself from the seat to wrap her arms around his neck. She felt the car jerk under her, but held on nevertheless, uncaring of accidental death or injury, as long as she could hang on to him. One more night was all they might have together. One more night to join as one, to be mates, to experience each other. Anxiety tore at her heart.

Desperation tore at his. Though barely able to see the road, he didn't push her away. He let her cling as he wanted to, but the danger stalking her wouldn't allow him to delay. His task was to get her to her brother, to safety, to freedom, even though that freedom would leave him in chains of despair. He reached up to squeeze her arm in reassurance. "We'll stop for something to eat in Sioux Falls and then try to drive on through the night."

Fighting for the control he had grasped, she slowly released him, pausing only to press a kiss against his whiskered cheek. To love was to feel pain, but to feel such pain was to live. She wouldn't regret what time they'd had any more than she would waste what little they had left. "You will buy me some more ice cream?"

"Absolutely."

She laughed, and he joined her. The joy of the moment was something they silently agreed upon and needed to hang on to.

"WHERE'RE YOU FOLKS headed from here?"

Derek glanced up at the waitress filling his coffee cup at a restaurant off the freeway outside Sioux Falls. It was early evening. Across from him, Kristiana sat quietly devouring a piece of apple pie à la mode. He couldn't see her face. It was hidden by the bill of the cap she had her hair tucked into. It wasn't much of a disguise, but it was all he'd been able to think of. He grinned at the top of the cap and turned back to the waitress. "Chicago."

She grunted. "Good thing you're going east instead of west."

"Why's that?" Derek asked, comfortable with his lying to protect Kristiana.

"Big spring storm coming in off the Rockies," the woman answered with a defeated sigh. "They expect we'll get at least half a foot of snow before it's over."

"Just when you thought you could put the snow shovels away," Derek murmured in sympathy, but his eyes turned to find Kristiana's as the waitress moved away.

Intrigued by the weather prediction, Kristiana looked from him out the window to the blue sky dimming with the end of day. "We will see snow?"

He couldn't miss the note of excitement that came into her voice. "You like snow?"

"I have seen it only in the ports." She shrugged. "Often all we see of different planets is what is at the space docks. Our trading usually keeps us busy within the one city. It is rare we get to go beyond or have free time to explore because we must return home quickly with our goods. Once when we visited Manox, the snow world, it snowed when I was outside the port."

"You don't have snow on Takyam?"

"Not where I live." She sighed. "The children on Manox seemed to be having great fun with the snow. I wished to join them."

"If we see some, I promise, we'll stop to let you play in it—maybe even build a snowman."

Her smile of delight had his stomach somersaulting and desire skyrocketing, and his heated response had her heart skipping and color staining her cheeks. But she didn't look away from his golden gaze. Instead, she leaned closer to whisper.

"We will do that again soon, too."

Startled at having his thoughts so easily read, Derek opened his mouth to protest but ended up grinning instead. "I can't wait. Done with that pie?"

"Almost." She finished with a few swallows. Still licking her lips as they returned to the car, she abruptly found herself pulled to him.

"I want to taste, too," he said, pulling the cap from her head to release the silken strands of her golden hair.

His murmur was all the encouragement she needed to press herself against him, where she was held in a tight embrace that had her toes curling in her shoes and her bones turning to water. She sighed as he released her. "You make me feel quite wonderful."

"Do I?"

"Kiss me again."

It was an order he couldn't refuse, not with the way she seemed to blend into him when he held her. The length of her body simply melted into his. He didn't know where she ended and he began. Tracing her lips with his tongue as he let her go, he echoed her earlier sigh. "That was good pie."

"I like you better."

Her response had a hard knot forming in his stomach and the temptation was strong to find a motel early, but destiny couldn't wait. Yet he thought he could delay it just a little.

Before leaving the city, he dragged a "disguised" Kristiana into a department store in search of mittens, jackets and winter wear—things not easily found when summer shorts and swimsuits filled the racks. But a few seasonal leftovers combined with some sporting goods provided them both with ensembles for the storm they would be heading into.

"Tell me how Roham waits," Derek said once they were back in the car and heading for the freeway exit.

Kristiana, having tossed the confining baseball cap onto the back seat, was eagerly riffling through the bags, fingering the fabrics of clothes the likes of which she'd never worn before. "How do you mean?"

"If the government knows Roham is waiting for us in Wyoming—and they might—how can he hide from them?"

"He will use the cloaking device that allows us to hide our ships when we come to Earth," she answered, closing the bag on her lap.

"You must have to land your crafts a long way from any city, then, when you come here to visit."

"We find a place that is close to where we wish to go, but not where a ship can be easily discovered. A deserted field, perhaps. Then we walk into the city to observe."

"But if it's dangerous to come here, why do you risk it at all?"

"We do not risk it often . . . for our own sake as well as yours," she said, putting the bags aside and curling up in her seat. "We do not want to cause trouble on your world, which our presence on Earth would certainly do if we were discovered. But we mean no harm. We are only interested in studying Earth's progress because of the similarities between our peoples."

Intrigued, Derek momentarily took his eyes from the road to glance at her in the shadowed confines of the car. "Tell me more about these similarities."

She smiled at him. "We have much in common, our worlds. It has always fascinated us. From two like beginnings, we have each taken different and yet parallel paths."

"How so?" Derek asked, his eyes back on the road as he took the exit onto the freeway.

"We began much the same, evolving, building cities, making alliances with some neighbors, going to war with others." She paused. "On our planet, our disputes were not always dissimilar to yours. Your history shows America fought over the enslavement of a race by another of Earth's countries. This we could not have because we have only one race on Takyam. But we, too, have had those who wish to maintain power over others."

"Rule the world?"

"Yes. But when we were forced to recognize we needed one another to survive, a peace came and a lifestyle developed that bound all our world together. It is difficult for me to believe now that we would ever have an interworld conflict again."

"And yet, on Earth we have many."

"Until you have a joint cause to bind you, it will probably always be so." She shrugged. "Yet, despite your conflicts—sometimes even because of them—your technology is closely following ours. Your communications and space explorations. Your work with cleaning the environment. These are stages we, too, went through."

"But medicine . . ."

"I have told you that it is not a perfect world. Progress for us in this field has been set aside by more urgent demands." She shook her head. "Many suffer. Entire communities can sometimes be lost to illness. It will come, in time, that we can cure sickness as we have helped our world recover from the damage we inflicted on it. I only wish we had someone who could show us the way."

"I'd like to help."

She smiled. "You would make medicine for us?"

Derek frowned as he considered. "If, somehow, we— Earth—could arrange to trade..." Then he could see her again, be with her. But even as he thought of the possibility, he knew it couldn't happen. Earth wasn't ready.

Too much fear, too much uncertainty, too much distrust of differences still existed. While benefits certainly could be gained by both sides, one side had yet to conquer its own demons before reaching out to—or even accepting the hand of—the other.

Understanding his thoughts, she touched his arm. "I will try to come back."

Derek's expression darkened. "You're not gone yet."

Chapter Fourteen

The snow started halfway to Rapid City, which was a little more than halfway to their destination—Sheridan, Wyoming. Mere flurries at first, the flakes grew thicker, heavier, fatter and more frequent the farther west they traveled.

Kristiana watched the pavement turn from merely wet to white as the snow started to stick, first to the grass, bushes and the trees, and then to the asphalt itself. In the beams of the headlights she watched as the flakes started to blow and listened as the wind began to whistle. It seemed an ominous sign for what was to come. And when she started to shake with the growing chill in the air, Derek ordered her into the clothes they'd just bought.

Turning up the heater against the clinging dampness, Derek tried to keep his eyes on the road and off her white flesh that was briefly exposed before being covered with a sweater and jacket. Visibility was getting worse, and common sense dictated that he stop, but his analytical mind argued the merits of staying on the move.

The storm was actually a blessing in disguise. It would make the government's search harder. It would tie up law-enforcement officials with countless weather-related problems, including road clearing and the inevitable fenderbenders, that would prevent deputies and sheriffs from watching for two people on the run. Thus, the storm would buy him time to cross the last state to get Kristiana closer to safety.

Hurrying would also see her leave him more quickly, but he wasn't going to use the storm as an excuse to stop. That type of selfishness had almost gotten her caught at the zoo. He wouldn't give in to the luxury of indulging himself. Not again. He wouldn't repeat the mistake that had put her at risk. Instead he continued to drive doggedly on, fighting the slick pavement pulling at the wheels, the flakes crowding the windshield and the cold gnawing at his body and his heart. Until her hand slipped over his.

"You must stop and change." Under hers, Derek's skin was cool to the touch, and he was tense. She could see it in the frown on his face as he stared at the whirling mass of white beyond the windshield and feel it in his hand as he gripped the wheel with ferocious intensity. Anxiety was making him push himself beyond the physical limits. Caring for her made it urgent that he keep her safe, but she could sense the conflict his feelings created. He wanted her to stay, yet he had to make sure she was quick to go.

Reluctantly pulling off to the side of the road, knowing she was right, he reached for the jacket, hat and gloves waiting for him in the bags on the back seat and put them on. "Are you warm enough?"

She nodded. The vehicle's heating device kept the chill outside largely at bay. If she was cold at all, it was on the inside, and that was mild discomfort compared to what he was enduring for her. When he turned back, ready to put the car in gear once more, worry made her stop him again. "You must rest."

"I'm fine." But her hand wouldn't release his, and she forced him to look at her.

"You are tired."

His smile was weary as his gloved fingers entwined themselves with hers. "Stop reading my mind. I didn't invite you in." Nevertheless, he leaned toward her, and she met him halfway.

The kiss, as always, made her heart flutter, her skin tingle, and her breath catch.

He pulled back to rub his nose against hers. "This is how our Eskimo kiss."

"It is?" Her eyes widened, and his smile grew.

"And this is how they keep warm on cold winter nights." He pulled her across the gap between their seats and into his lap, turning her into his arms.

Surprised delight had her opening her mouth to his gentle conquest—and giggling under his suddenly playful nuzzles and nips. It was a game she quickly learned to participate in as she kissed his ears and his nose before nibbling at his throat. She squealed when he rubbed his whiskers across her bare skin and ended up leaning on the horn.

The loud toot had her jumping back against him, and he caught her with a laugh. "Making out in cars does have its liabilities."

"'Making out'?" she repeated.

"What we're doing. It's slang for necking." And at her puzzled expression, he added, "Kissing, hugging, or otherwise fooling around with a member of the opposite sex." He kissed her again. "It's generally frowned upon, especially when you steam up the windows."

She looked at the glass surrounding them and the fog clinging to it. "What do the Eskimo do to prevent this?"

"I don't think they care." He didn't think he did, either. With the way she was squirming in his lap, he could easily be convinced to completely forget where he was—cramped quarters or not.

She laughed and caught his face between her hands. "I think I like to act like an Eskimo."

"Me, too." His head descended toward hers again, but a huge semitrailer suddenly thundered past, pelting the Firebird with a blast of wind and a sea of slush. It made the car shake and Derek sigh. Reluctantly urging her back to her seat, he turned to the wheel once more. "We have to keep going."

But it wasn't a journey he or Kristiana enjoyed. Despite the best efforts of plow and salt truck, the snow built up until three lanes of traffic were whittled down to one. Near midnight that wasn't too much of a problem—between the late hour and the howling storm, few vehicles were on the road—but Derek was determined to get Rapid City behind them.

In good weather and with an alert mind, he estimated the drive should be just over seven hours from one side of the state to the other. In bad weather, and fighting to stay awake, he was engaged in a battle that Mother Nature would inevitably make him lose.

Nosing the car through a drift blown across an exit ramp, he headed for a neon sign that read Oasis Motel. And it was an oasis, albeit a single building in the midst of a blur of white.

After pulling into what he hoped was a parking spot, he left Kristiana in the car and headed for the motel office.

When he returned with the key, she wasn't huddled inside waiting for him. She was playing in the snow.

Running through it, falling in it, throwing it in the air, she stopped only to open her mouth to the sky to try to catch some of the whirling flakes on her tongue. Derek shivered against the cold, but she seemed oblivious. She continued to romp. He grinned and shoved the room key into his pocket before bending to scoop up a handful of the wet white stuff.

Kristiana cried out when something hit her in the back. It didn't cause so much pain as shock, and she whirled to find Derek—laughing at her. She laughed, too, and ducked when he threw his next missile.

A mad chase through the snowdrifts ensued, filled with laughter and screams of mock outrage as they romped in carefree abandon. Derek stopped the play to keep his promise. He started building a snowman, and Kristiana was quick to help once she caught on to what he was doing. Even though their "Frosty" didn't have any coal for his eyes or a carrot for his nose, she was delighted with the result.

And she was just as excited about learning to make snow angels. After some instructions—and a demonstration—she made a row of them to admire.

She soon discovered that not everything about snow was fun. Derek's icy face wash was something she was sure she could live without, along with the feel of icecold snow sliding down her collar. But neither truly dimmed her enthusiasm—or his. They continued to run, slide and roll, their cavorting as timeless as child's play, until the cold and the wet finally drove them to seek shelter.

Plodding to their room, soaked to the skin and numb, they warmed up quickly enough when Derek walked through the motel door behind her and was greeted by her greedy lips.

"You're all wet," he told her when he came up for air. "You need to get out of these clothes."

She grinned. "Then you will take me for another shower?"

"Like that Earth tradition, do you?"

She tugged him toward the bathroom as he managed to unzip his jacket.

"I'll beat you in," he challenged.

"You will not!"

Clothes and snow flew as they raced each other out of soggy jackets and sodden shoes. Drenched jeans and socks were quick to follow, making an unruly path across the floor to the door.

The first burst of water that caught them was cold. It had her squealing as her numbed feet danced on cold porcelain, but heat was quick to follow. From him for her. His body heated hers even as steam started to cloud the air.

A bar of soap was found and unwrapped. In Derek's clever hands it made her slick as well as clean, and she shared the suds with him as her flesh rubbed against his in a mad groping match that ended on a satisfied cry.

The towels provided tools for a brisk rubdown that left hair and skin only partially dry before she was carried from the bathroom to the waiting bed. Cool sheets caught her heated body, and she was quick to drag him to them, too.

The exploration was without wonder this time. It was filled with intense longings to please and be pleased, to seek out and find those places that stimulated, to eliminate those that did not. The assault was breathtaking, thorough, and all-consuming. Both thought it would

never end, that climax would never be reached because
neither was ready to give in until they could hold out no
more.

He filled, she surrounded, and each was buried in the
boundless giving of a love whose depth rivaled that of
couples who had come together thus for years. From
different worlds, joined, they were fulfilled, and in each
other's arms they slept until the urge to share in one
another had them waking again.

"TELL ME where you'll go when you leave."

Draped against Derek under the warm covers, Kristiana snuggled against the hard length of his body as
they lay in bed. Outside, the sun glared off fallen snow.
It was day. Derek wanted to leave, but the plows hadn't
cleared the way. Not yet. She didn't mind and didn't
think he really did, either. "We will return to the mother
ship, and from there go to Takyam."

"Is it a long journey?"

She heard the wonder in his voice and understood.
Traveling through space enthralled her still, even though
she had sped through it more times than memory allowed her to recall. "It is difficult to explain in Earth
time, but no. Three of your days, perhaps."

"Will your people be upset with you?"

"Because my ship was lost?" She moved one shoulder, enjoying the feel of his fingers tangling in the length
of her hair. "It could not be helped. Something went
wrong."

"Can you find out what so it doesn't happen again?"
He didn't want her crashing somewhere else. The next
time she might not be lucky enough to escape the
flames....

"The beacon that carried my message will also have all the computer information. We should be able to discover what caused the ship to malfunction."

"I'm glad."

"You are worried for me?"

Her smile was teasing, and he caught her chin as it hovered above his chest. "You bet."

His lips were warm and sure, and she melded hers to them with a sigh.

He let her snuggle against him, but his curiosity didn't end. Not for her or for what her life was like. He wanted—needed—to understand the everyday routine he would never be able to share with her. "What about after you get home? What will you do then?"

Think of him. Wonder where he was. She pushed the thoughts and pain aside. "See my family. Prepare to go on another trading run."

"So soon?"

"There is no reason to stay at home. I am free to come and go as I please, and I enjoy the commerce. It is my job." And it would keep her busy. She would have no time to grieve for what she had enjoyed briefly and too quickly lost.

"You shouldn't be free."

Startled by his comment, she raised her head to meet his pensive stare.

"You should have someone to go home to. Someone waiting for you."

"A mate?" She shook her head. "That is no longer possible."

He frowned. "Why not?"

"I have mated with you."

Stunned, he lay silent. The implication was clear but, for her sake, he didn't want to believe it. "Explain."

"You are my mate. There can be no other."

Abruptly he sat up, bringing her with him. "Are you saying that because you've 'mated' with me, you're going to spend the rest of your life alone? You'll never take a husband?"

She shrugged. "On Takyam, when we mate, we mate for life. It is our way."

Speechless, Derek dragged a hand through his hair and tried to grasp what she was telling him. For her, he was her first. And last.

"From birth we are raised to look forward to the joining. We learn about our bodies and of the pleasure to be shared between mates. It is something we are schooled in, for being prepared for union is to share more joy with each other."

"None of you ever...there's never any..." He took a deep breath to steady himself. "On your planet there is no 'joining' before marriage?"

Matter-of-factly, she shook her head. "Not for most. Of course, with the mixing of worlds comes the mixing of ways. Other rituals now blend with ours. We accept those changes."

"But you...you believe there is only one mate for life?"

"It is a way to honor the one we love."

"But what about accidents, illness, death?" he tried, desperate to undo the wrong he'd done. By indulging himself, he had robbed her of the companionship she deserved. And he'd robbed her of it for the rest of her life.

"Some will join again."

He grasped her shoulders. "Kristiana, I don't want you to be alone. I never... You didn't tell me... I didn't ask." He let her go. "How could I be so stupid? Your questions." Too late, he remembered. He should have guessed. Should have asked. Had wanted to, but hadn't.

Sensing his distress, she stopped him when he would have turned away from her to leave the bed. "Please do not be angry with me. I did not think it would matter. Your Earth rituals..."

His eyes met hers. "You're not from Earth." Her gaze fell, and he sighed. "And I'm not angry. Not with you."

Blue met gold once more, and when he held out his arms, she slid into them.

"I don't want you to be alone, Kristiana. You deserve better." He held her close as she trembled, and he wondered. Even if she'd told him, if he'd understood the implications of her loving him, would he have been able to resist her? "Is it forbidden for a woman on Takyam who has...joined as you and I have to take a mate?"

"No." She bit her lip. "It would be accepted."

"But?" he prodded, hearing the reservation in her voice.

"You and I are different. The council will not be happy."

He nodded immediate understanding. "Because Earth is not ready." He sighed again and cursed his own lack of willpower. "Will you be in trouble because of me?"

Enjoying the steady rhythm of the beat of his heart beneath her ear, she smiled. "I do not think they can be too unhappy. The crash landing was not planned, and neither were you."

He laughed and sank back with her onto the pillows once more. "I wasn't expecting you, either."

"You are disappointed?" she asked, smiling down at him as she leaned on one elbow beside him.

"You're a lot better looking than the little green men I've always heard about."

She frowned. "Little green men?"

"The ones who are supposed to live on Mars."

Her frown deepened. "But Mars—"

He put a finger to her lips. "It's an expression."

She sighed. "I do not think I will ever understand all these expressions."

His gaze locked with hers, and his hand clutched a fistful of golden-white hair. "I want you to think about taking another mate." It hurt even to suggest it. It drove him crazy to think of any other man touching her. But the alternative, for her to wander space endlessly with only an empty home to return to for the rest of her life... He knew what being alone was like. The silent house, the unshared thoughts, the wasted dreams.

"You will take one?"

The question took him by surprise, and the pain in her eyes reflected what he felt. He brought her back down to him. "Kristiana, what have we done to each other?"

She rested against him. "Perhaps I can return to live in your California."

His heart jumped at the possibility and at her willingness to try. She'd sacrifice her world for him, give up all she had to be with him—but could he possibly keep her? Once she left him, would the government ever leave him alone? Or would they monitor him for the rest of his life, watching for her return?

Anger flared. His life would never be the same. Not after she was gone. He'd never be this complete again.

Abruptly he rolled to pin her beneath him, and she met his embrace eagerly. If his lips were harsh, if suppressed fury lingered in his touch, she knew it wasn't for her. His frustration was at the impossibility of their situation—and it matched hers. As did his need for her. She wanted him, too. For as long as she could have him.

Desperation fired passion this time. Gentleness was lost as greed and fear overtook love and desire. The angry emotions tossed them around the bed, tangling sheets with limbs, making breath sharp, need great and union hasty. Love's aftermath left little satisfaction. The need was still there. The anxiety. Time was running out.

Ignoring it, they tried to make it stop by clinging to each other again, but they couldn't beat the clock. Disappointment was bitter, and as he collapsed once more beside her, Derek realized the great Virgil had been wrong. Love didn't conquer all. Love wasn't even enough to keep the woman he loved beside him.

IT WAS LATE AFTERNOON when they left the motel. Sleep had taken them for a while, lovemaking for as much time as dared be claimed. But wanting to deny it wouldn't stop the day of parting from coming to pass. The end was very near.

Behind the wheel and on the highway once more, as Kristiana sat silently beside him in the car, Derek tried to convince himself that, once it was over, he would be better for the experience. For a short time at least, he had enjoyed a love most men would never know. An old saying kept bouncing around in his head to confirm that belief. Something about it being better to have loved and lost than never to have loved at all. But all his reasoning and old words of wisdom brought him little consolation.

For him the future looked as bleak as the countryside, buried in a whiteness that left the landscape barren of life. He could find in the fading day's sun only one bright spot. The hope that she would return. For in that possibility, he was sure, was his sole chance of ever seeing her again. Earth would not be ready for travel in space—or for more than an unannounced visit from extraterrestrials—for a very long time.

Signs appeared to announce the coming and then the going of Rapid City, and the snow cover began to disappear as the Firebird neared the Dakota state line. Wyoming lay just ahead, but Derek chose not to break the quiet in the car. No joy would come from announcing that just five hours away lay Sheridan, and a waiting Roham.

Instead, pushing aside thoughts of parting from Kristiana, he tried to focus on what her brother would be like. Certainly, in appearance, Roham would resemble his sister. But what would be his nature? Would he, too, lack guile and see the world—the universe—with accepting innocence? Or would his years of space travel, his greater age, make him more jaded—perhaps more like the human his sister had bonded with?

Derek glanced at Kristiana and found her sitting with her eyes closed and her head back against the seat. What would Roham say when he found out she'd taken an Earthly mate?

Derek smothered a sigh and returned his attention to the road, unconcerned with brotherly anger or the possibility of retribution. He didn't regret what had passed between Kristiana and him, even though knowing she would remain his gave him pause.

Selfishly, humanly, he was glad she wouldn't actively be seeking a mate, someone to replace him in her life. It reassured him that she wouldn't forget him any more than he'd ever forget her. Still, he worried that she would have no one to look after her, to share life, to love her as she deserved to be loved.

Absently noting the fuel gage was dipping toward empty, Derek guided the Pontiac off the highway toward a service station. It was Sunday. If he didn't fill up before the sun set, it was unlikely that he'd find an open station later on. Stopping at the pumps, he climbed from the car and began to uncap the tank. But fuel became the least of his concerns when he looked up to see Kristiana get out of the car.

She had been remarkably quiet all afternoon. She hadn't tried to interrupt his thoughts or to make conversation even once. He'd assumed her silence meant she, too, was searching for consequences of their union and thinking about leaving Earth. As she weaved on her feet, he dropped the gas cap and ran to her side.

"Kristiana, what is it?"

"I feel..."

Her knees buckled, and he caught her with an oath. Setting her back into the passenger seat, he noted her flushed face. Shaking off his glove, his hand found her forehead hot. His heart thudded against his chest in alarm as he stared down at her. She was burning up!

Chapter Fifteen

Going any farther was out of the question. After filling up and paying for the gas, Derek headed for the first motel he saw, and left Kristiana there, buried under a mound of blankets while he went in search of an open drugstore. He found one a few miles away.

Pacing its aisles, he pounded his brain for what he should buy. While Kristiana's body makeup appeared the same as that of any other female's on Earth's, he didn't know if there were subtle chemical differences that might be adversely affected by the simplest of man-made medicines. Relying on what he did know and on what he believed—that for every illness on Earth there was a natural cure—he did the best he could with what the pharmacy had to offer.

Aspirin was his first choice. An Earth medicine Kristiana had already used and endured, it would be good for fighting fever and inflammation. He chose the largest bottle he could find. Vitamin C was his second selection. A stethoscope and a thermometer also fell prey to his questing grip. But as he struggled to find other over-the-counter organic solutions, he kept hitting dead ends. Until he stumbled across a bottle of castor oil....

Misguidedly consigned a reputation linked with punishment, Derek knew that the healing powers of castor oil were extensive—even if no one could completely understand how or why. The oil had mysteriously helped cure ailments from simple nausea to congestion, not to mention actual physical injuries.

Emptying the shelf of the oil, he checked out with his haul, which included a hot plate for boiling the water he'd need to make the soup, broth and coffee he intended to purchase at the grocery store down the block. The soup and broth were for Kristiana. The coffee was for him. He had the feeling he was going to need it.

When he reached the motel room, Kristiana was sleeping fitfully. The blankets had been tossed aside as her fever raged. He set the bags down to pull the covers over her once more, and she woke immediately.

"Hot." The word was a mumble and her gaze was clouded and unfocused.

"I know you're hot, but you have to keep the blankets on. We have to break the fever. Do you understand?"

His voice was a salve, comforting as his hand on her forehead was cooling. "I am dying?"

His heart jumped against his ribs, but he met the blue eyes that stared up at him with a reassuring smile. "You may feel that way, but you're not ready to bite the dust yet."

"Bite..."

"Another expression." Her smile was weak, and he bent to press his lips to her burning cheek. "I'm going to give you some medicine, and you're going to get well.''

Night fell over the motel and the town he didn't know, but Derek was barely aware of the passage of time as he pumped Kristiana full of aspirin and vitamin C and ripped his newly purchased flannel shirt into strips to make a castor oil pack.

When she'd fallen ill, his first reaction had been that the wound on her arm that he'd thought to be healing had somehow become infected. But it wasn't her arm causing the fever. The cut was nearly completed healed. He suspected what had struck her down was a little something Earthlings called the flu. The affliction was generally as harmless as it was miserable, but Derek knew that it could turn deadly on an unlucky few.

Though he silently worried, his stethoscope and thermometer assured him that her vital signs remained strong and as normal as his—except for a temperature that seemed determined to continue to climb. He did what he could to help her fight the virus via medication and nourishment, but as the hours passed and the infection spread, she began resisting his attempts to give her broth or liquids. Her throat and lymph nodes were swollen, making it painful for her to swallow. Her slim, supple body filled with aches, and her skin remained heated and flushed.

Gulping coffee to keep himself alert, Derek sat by her bed as the fever rose and she tossed restlessly, the sheets becoming soaked with her sweat. He fought to keep her under the covers and warm despite her body's inner heat. But the number of blankets on the bed increased when her teeth started to chatter and her skin went cold and clammy.

Climbing under the covers with her, he held her close as tremors shook her every limb. Recognition was stolen by the illness holding her intently in its grip. She didn't know who he was anymore, and he didn't try to explain. He simply kept his arms around her as she fought the demons the fever had unleashed.

Words he didn't understand, places he'd never heard of, were mumbled whispers on her lips. Her temperature stayed high as the heat returned to burn her body. He climbed out of bed to try to pour more aspirin and liquids down her scorched throat. He was only partially successful.

MORNING CAME with a burst of sunlight just beyond the drawn curtains, but Derek didn't notice. With his head in his hands, he racked his already weary brain for other solutions, other alternatives. That the fever had stopped climbing—had, actually dropped to ninety-nine—was good. What he was doing was working, but was it enough?

The only other learned skill he could think of to use was an ancient technique from China. He'd never studied or used the needles of acupuncture, but he understood shiatsu. He knew that the pressure could be just as effective as using a needle. He returned to the bed and Kristiana to ply the curative technique.

His touch seemed to reach beyond the fever. Her eyes fluttered open to stare mindlessly into his for a long moment, and he held his breath for some sign that what he was doing was right.

"You would have made a good doctor."

His smile and his hands trembled with relief at the hoarse whisper. "How do you feel?"

Confusion clouded her gaze, and he bent to press his lips to hers briefly. "You're getting better."

"Better," she repeated, and her eyelids drooped. "Tired."

"Sleep, then." It took less than an instant for her to slip away from him again. The loss of consciousness came so quickly, it nearly took his breath away, but she was still breathing, and the thermometer said her temperature remained only slightly elevated.

Relief had him standing to stretch, but a black wave of dizziness had him groping for a chair. Alarmed, surprised and frightened by his own body's weakness, Derek froze, to collect his strength. Finally, the sun beyond the curtains caught his eye. He glanced at his watch. The time told him why tremors were making his knees shake. He needed food. A few strides took him to the phone on the scarred dresser.

"Desk."

"Yes, this is room eleven," Derek told the anonymous male on the other end of the line. He continued to watch Kristiana. "My...my wife, isn't feeling well, and I don't want to leave her. I wonder if I could have some sandwiches brought in. Is there a place I can call that delivers?"

A mumbled reply of compliance came quickly. But once he'd hung up and moved back to the bed, Derek was flooded with surprising warmth. He put out a hand to brush Kristiana's forehead. "My wife," he told her quietly, recognizing the truth of the statement. Even without any formal ceremony, she was his and he was hers, whether or not space kept them apart. "My mate."

She didn't hear him, but the wonder and the smile that came to his lips remained as he answered the knock at the door less than a half hour later.

The man standing outside, bundled up against the weather was the same man who had checked Derek in. He held up a bag for Derek to view. "I hope this will do it. I had my wife make some sandwiches, and she sent along a thermos of tea for your wife."

"Thank you," Derek said, accepting the bag and the bottle. "Thank your wife, too. She's very kind."

The man glanced into the shadowed room. "She had the flu herself not too long ago. She remembers how bad it was. Mean bug this year."

Derek glanced back into the room, too. "Very mean."

"You want I should call a doctor? You being from out of town and all . . ."

Derek almost said yes because he desperately wanted a professional opinion and the use of a laboratory. But he couldn't chance it. Calling a doctor would put Kristiana into the very hands he was trying to keep her out of, for any physician who examined her would most assuredly notice her body's unique organ alignments and would sound the alarm. So instead of gratefully accepting the offer of assistance, Derek pulled the stethoscope from his pants' pocket and grinned wryly.

The man laughed and left with a wave. Twice more before nightfall he came to the door with more sandwiches, tea and sympathy, leaving the last time just before Kristiana's fever suddenly spiked again.

The quiet afternoon that had allowed her to sleep and Derek to doze was abruptly forgotten as he jumped to do battle with the virus once again. His efforts were quick and sure—more liquids and aspirin combined with castor oil and acupressure—to wage war, but his foe wasn't about to let go. Kristiana's temperature continued to climb.

Derek began cursing himself, his lack of ability, and his stupidity for allowing her to romp in the snow. Earth humans caught colds for doing less. What had he been thinking of?

Guilt was a bitter companion, and it offered no comfort as fear came to hold him in a cruel grip. The fever was still nudging the thermometer upward. He was losing the fight, and all too clearly memory brought forth the face of the man who'd died in his arms years before when he had been a medical student determined to save the world....

Somewhere in the night, exhaustion caused mindless collapse. Though sitting steadfastly in the chair beside the bed, Derek fell asleep, waking with a start hours later when, outside, a car door slammed and an engine started.

He was on his knees beside the bed instantly, searching for a pulse. It came firm and strong. And the skin he touched was no longer hot. Holding his breath, he put the back of his hand to Kristiana's forehead, and tears of joy nearly blinded him. The fever had broken!

Blue eyes unexpectedly opened to look up into his, and the most wonderful smile he'd ever seen stretched across her lips. His hand found hers beneath the blanket.

"You're awake," he murmured.

"You saved me."

He shook his head. "I think you've got that backward. It's the other way around. You saved me." From a life of false fulfillment, from a house brimming with memories, from a bone-deep loneliness he hadn't recognized until now. "How do you feel?"

She frowned and tried to find the aches, the pain that had been twisting her body into agonizing spasms. But they were gone, leaving her drained, weak and... "Hungry."

He laughed and kissed her fingers. "You do like Earth food, don't you?" But even as he watched, her eyelids drifted closed. "I think you'd better get some rest first."

She didn't argue. She just smiled as sleep swiftly carried her into the deep slumber of recovery.

Watching her give in to the healing wave of fatigue, Derek blinked as tears threatened to blur his vision. This patient, he hadn't lost.

A knock sounded at the door and Derek swiftly rose to his feet. Kristiana wasn't the only one who was hungry, and it sounded as if the motel manager was back. Derek eagerly reached for the knob, but the man he found standing outside wasn't the one he'd been expecting to see. Derek felt his stomach drop to his knees. "Rogers."

The government agent didn't wait to be invited inside. He merely strode in, with Tony Magrini right behind him. "You gave us one hell of a race. Why'd you stop here?"

Derek's jaw and mind worked silently as he shut the door and turned to answer. "Because she's dying." The silence that followed his declaration was effective. It gave him the precious moments he needed to think. "A bad case of the flu. It can kill Earth humans. You can imagine what it's doing to her."

Watching Derek move to a chair by the bed, Rogers had no reason to doubt the answer. The dark room, the bottles of medicine, and the blankets mounded on the bed all spoke of serious illness with an indefinable air of quiet. Not to mention Derek's appearance. He'd obviously been in the same clothes for days, and he looked scruffy with a rough growth of whiskers lining his jaw.

"We can get a doctor," Magrini offered, stepping forward to stare down at the woman sleeping in the bed. She looked normal enough, in appearance, but fear had his skin crawling anyway. Fear of the unknown.

Derek once again lifted the stethoscope into view.

"An ambulance, then," Rogers offered, filled more with awe than with worry at actually being in the presence of a humanoid from another planet.

"I don't want her moved," Derek argued. "She's warm here. Safe."

"Medicine—" Rogers started to say but stopped when Derek shook his head.

"I don't know what I can give her. No one would, without extensive tests, and I don't think we have that much time."

"It's that bad?" Rogers asked, moving closer even as Magrini suddenly backed up.

"Maybe she brought some disease with her," the redhead said.

Derek turned to glare at Magrini. "Find any bodies where she's been, Magrini? I've been with her for days, and I'm not dead yet."

"There've been no reports of any unusual illness," Rogers quickly agreed, with a frown at his partner.

"And there won't be," Derek declared. "She's not here to hurt anybody. She's here by accident. Her ship crashed. The only thing she wants to do is go home."

"You're on the way to meet her people," Rogers stated rather than asked.

"And we would have made it if it hadn't been for that trooper in Nebraska who pulled us over," Derek told him with an angry glare. "We would have gone straight through to Casper rather than having to head north."

"Casper?" Magrini asked, suddenly interested again.

Derek spared him no more than a glance, determined not to put Roham at risk. Cloaking or no cloaking device, he was going to keep the government dogs away from where Kristiana had been—and was still going. "You'll never find them."

"We'll try," Magrini declared, and strode out of the room.

Rogers stayed at the foot of the bed. "That trooper was the one who led us to you."

Derek raised a questioning brow.

"The garage. The Pontiac was called in as stolen. The officer investigating the theft recognized the car you dumped from an all-points bulletin issued earlier by a fellow officer whose squad car had apparently taken on a life of its own." Rogers shrugged. "It didn't take much deduction."

"Two plus two," Derek murmured, and looked at Kristiana, praying she wouldn't suddenly awaken. He had to warn her first.

"How'd she do it?"

"Do what?"

"Move the squad car."

Derek grinned. "Telekinesis."

Rogers grinned, too. "No kidding." He nodded to her. "What's she like?"

Derek shrugged. "Like you and me. She walks and talks, breathes, bleeds, and catches the flu. She even gets scared. That's how she moved the car."

"Fear?"

"Yes, fear of being caught and caged," Derek said, standing again. "Imagine how it would feel, Rogers, being somewhere you don't want to be, somewhere where nothing and no one is familiar. You don't know where to go, what to do, who to trust. The only thing that keeps you alive is the hope of rescue, of going home."

"We don't want to hurt her."

"You only want to lock her up, put her in a lab where you can draw blood and take pictures." Derek took a step closer. "How'd you like to be part of a zoo, Rogers? Think you'd enjoy it?"

"I'm just doing my job."

"Really?" Derek lifted an eyebrow. "Get a good pension for locking up dangerous people like her?"

The door opened, and Magrini came back in. "They're sending a van from the nearest base. It'll be here tomorrow morning."

"Better check us into the room next door, then," Rogers told him, and Magrini nodded and left again. "You look like you could use a shower and a shave, Carpenter."

Derek grunted and moved around him to the dresser. "What day is it, anyway?"

"Tuesday."

Derek glanced at his watch. "Any problem with my phoning the office? Now that you know where I am, I don't have to worry about your tracing my call."

Rogers shrugged and crossed the room to sit in a chair where he could keep an eye on everything and everyone but remain out of the way. "Be my guest."

It was only moments before David's voice came over the line. "Derek? Is it really you?"

Derek grinned at the tone of anxious disbelief. "It's me."

"Where are you? What's happening? Where's Kristiana? Did she get off okay? When are you coming back?"

"Which question would you like me to answer first?"

David laughed. "Sorry."

Derek looked from Rogers to Kristiana, his mind working, searching for a plan. "I'm in a little motel just outside Rapid City. The Buffalo Bill Inn. Kristiana and I were on our way to Wyoming when she got sick."

"Sick! Is she all right?"

"The feds found us at the inn," Derek continued as if David hadn't spoken.

"The . . . They're there now?"

"Both your friends are."

David swore. "Kristiana?"

"Sleeping. She doesn't know yet."

"Great." Silence followed. "What can I do?"

"Nothing but pay your taxes. What's happening there?"

"We're okay. The government finally left us to plague someone else. What are you going to do?"

"I'm not sure."

"Derek . . ."

"I'm all right. Better than all right," Derek interrupted, not wanting to hear the warnings and the cautions. He knew what he had to do. It only remained to be seen how he'd do it.

"I'll fly out and pick you up. It sounds like you might need a friend."

"I don't know if our government buddies will let me go with you. Besides, I can't leave yet. Kristiana needs me."

Something in his tone of voice told David more than words. "I'm still coming. I probably won't get there until tonight. Just don't let them move you before I arrive."

"It won't be them."

"What do you mean? They're not moving... Wait a minute. You're talking about you. Derek, don't do anything stupid."

"Not stupid, just necessary."

"Derek..."

"See you, friend."

David's mouth went dry, recognizing the tone of a goodbye when he heard it. A final one, at that. "Derek..."

Derek hung up and looked at Rogers. "My partner's flying out in the company jet. Says he'll be here tonight. Any problem with that?"

Rogers shook his head. "The more, the merrier."

Derek walked back to the bedside, dragging a hand through his hair and otherwise acting weary before bending to put a hand to Kristiana's forehead. He straightened to look at the small table behind him loaded with bottles and cups and patted his pants' pockets as if searching for something. "You see the stethoscope?"

"You left it by the phone," Rogers said, rising and moving toward it.

Derek waited where he was. "Thanks," he acknowledged as he took the instrument with his right hand before swiftly and silently swinging with his left.

Rogers was unconscious before he hit the floor.

Derek winced and brought his knuckles to his lips before shaking his stinging hand. "One down." But he had to be ready when the second man came through the door.

Sneaking a quick look out the window from behind the drawn curtains, Derek saw Magrini coming down the walk from the office. He gritted his teeth and bent to swiftly search Rogers for a weapon. When he found it, he kicked Rogers's legs out of the way and took a position behind the door.

When it opened, the first thing Magrini saw was the bed and Kristiana. The second was Rogers stretched out on the floor. And the third was the wall as Derek grabbed his shirtfront and threw him into it. Instinct had Magrini immediately spinning and reaching for his gun, but he wasn't fast enough. Derek put the nose of Rogers's small revolver against Magrini's chin.

"Now, Magrini, you're going to help me."

"I'll die first," Magrini declared. "I'm not going to help you get that . . . thing out of here."

Derek's fingers tightened around Magrini's shirt. "That *thing* is a woman. A human being. She's not here to invade Earth. She's here by mistake, like I told you before, and all she wants to do is leave."

"She's staying."

Derek shoved the revolver up harder into Magrini's throat. "You have a choice." His finger pulled the gun's hammer back. "She's either going home, or you're going straight to hell."

Chapter Sixteen

"My wife's resting comfortably now," Derek told the motel manager as he paid for the extra day's stay. "I'm going to run out and stretch my legs for a while so she can sleep undisturbed. I really appreciate all the help you've given us."

"It was nothing. Glad I could give you a hand." The man beamed. "Like I said, when my wife got the flu..."

Derek smiled and appeared, at least, to listen intently, but he was more concerned with distracting the man's attention from what was happening outside. Kristiana was sneaking into the government vehicle parked in front of their motel room door.

The plan was for her to drive the sedan away. Once Derek got out of the motel office, he was to follow in the Pontiac. They would drive separate cars until they found a safe place to leave the flashy Firebird. It was easy to spot, and with a bulletin already out on it, Derek didn't want to take the chance on continuing to drive the sports car for fear the all clear hadn't yet reached every sheriff's station. They didn't have any time to waste, and he didn't want to risk being pulled over again. The next time they might not get away so easily.

Using the government vehicle to make the getaway to Wyoming would be safer.

Accepting a receipt for the room, Derek smiled again, waved and stepped out the door and into the noon hour sunlight. The first thing he looked for was the government sedan, but it was gone. Nodding to himself, he headed for the Pontiac, rubbing a hand over his cleanly shaven jaw. It had taken precious time to rid himself of the growing beard once he'd had both Rogers and Magrini bound and gagged, but he'd figured looking like vagabonds wouldn't help Kristiana and him.

On waking her, he'd gotten her into the shower while he shaved, and then he'd allowed himself a few luxurious minutes under a hot stream of water while she dressed. Refreshed and in clean clothes, they both felt better, but he was still worried about her. She needed a good meal and more rest. The fever had left her weak and susceptible. She belonged in bed, not on the road.

Slipping into and starting up the Firebird's engine, Derek couldn't help but grin at the motel door with the Do Not Disturb sign hung on the knob. Rogers and Magrini were inside, one stuck in the bathtub, the other trussed up like a stuffed chicken on the bed. His grin grew. It had given him a great deal of pleasure to drop Magrini into the tub.

Heading away from the motel and the immobilized government agents, Derek drove only a block before spotting Kristiana parked by the curb, waiting for him. As he passed, he motioned for her to follow him and kept an eye on her in the rearview mirror once she was behind him. His first priority after dumping the Pontiac was to get her some food. An empty stomach wasn't the way to fight off any lingering effects of the fever.

Kristiana was more than ready to eat when they stopped a short time later. Scraping her fork across her empty plate, she lifted it to lick the metal prongs with a contented sigh. The Pontiac had been left in a busy shopping center parking lot. The freeway and Sheridan lay ahead, and with her stomach full, all seemed well.

"Good?"

Looking up to find Derek watching her from across the table, she nodded emphatically. It seemed an eternity had passed since she'd eaten last, and every bite was like *bacara*, a very rare and very expensive Takyamian delicacy she seldom got to taste. "Very good," she assured him, oblivious to the nearly deserted highway diner but not to the grin that immediately spread across his lips. She smiled back and couldn't resist the urge to reach out and touch him.

During the fever, he had been all she'd had to hang on to. It had been his touch, his voice, that had guided her through the nightmares, beyond the frightening images and the pain, back to sanity. "I am glad you have shaved your beard. You are much more handsome without it."

"Is that so?" he asked, curling his fingers over hers. Her face was no longer flushed, her eyes no longer clouded, and her appetite told him that she'd shaken off the worst effects of the virus. She appeared as healthy as she had ever been—and as good enough to eat as anything on the menu. "How do you feel?"

Her free hand moved to her stomach. "Full."

"Then we'd better get going." But even as he said the words, he didn't want to leave, knowing that in mere hours she'd be gone.

"We are safe?"

He tightened his grip on her hand in reassurance as her eyes darkened in fear. "I think so." She had been as shocked upon waking to find the government agents in the motel room as he had been to find them at the door. "The backup Rogers and Magrini ordered isn't due until tomorrow morning. I disconnected and hid the phone so they can't call. The motel manager thinks you're resting, so no maid will go in. With any luck, it'll be morning by the time those two get someone's attention, and you'll be with Roham by then."

Joy and sorrow collided on the thought of her waiting brother. Joy to see him and to go home, but sorrow at leaving the man she'd chosen as her life mate. She forced a smile. "You will like him."

"I hope he likes me."

Her laugh as she reluctantly followed him from the table hid her concern. Would the two men closest to her have a chance to exchange more than a few words? Could they possibly have the opportunity to get to know each other even a little? How hasty would her goodbye have to be? Swallowing doubts and fears, she tried not to drag her feet on the way to the car and resisted the urge to ask Derek to stop once they got back on the freeway. Part of her didn't want to leave Earth. A very large part.

Feeling her eyes on him, Derek reached out with his right hand to entwine her fingers with his. He wasn't going to think about the future. He was going to focus on the present, on taking one minute at a time. She was still with him. But the press of minutes was relentless. And he was worried, even if he didn't tell her that he was.

Provided they were able to keep driving without detours and unnecessary stops, it was still a good five-hour run to Sheridan. In that time, anything could go wrong. Rogers and Magrini could be discovered, the government sedan could be called in as missing, and they could be caught. His fingers tightened on the steering wheel in silent determination. If he couldn't have her, he vowed, no one else on Earth would, either.

Not unaware of his thoughts, Kristiana drew his gaze to her by pulling gently on his hand. She had so much she wanted to say. Her entire life, she'd looked forward to finding her mate, someone to share and bond with, but now that she'd found him, she had to leave him behind. Her eyes locked with his, but all the words she wanted to say wouldn't come. Instead, she could only wrap both her hands around his free one as a wealth of emotion passed between them with a glance.

Derek turned his attention back to the road. His grip on hers was firm, and strong with silent understanding. She blinked back the tears she didn't want to shed and tried not to think or feel as mile after mile relentlessly disappeared behind them and brought her closer and closer to Sheridan and Roham.

WHEN THE CITY finally came into view, the remnants of the spring snowstorm had been left behind them and green grass could be seen in the shadows of the sun dipping toward the western horizon. Its dying rays reflected off a visitors center that loomed large and welcoming next to the highway. It seemed an appropriate place to stop, and Derek pulled off the freeway. Guiding the black sedan over the pavement, he pulled to a halt in the parking lot and cut the engine.

"Where to now?" he asked, looking out the windshield to the building and its surroundings. "How do we find Roham?"

"We cannot. He must find us."

Derek nodded, his gaze moving to her. "He'll know we're here?"

She nodded and tried to smile, but as hopelessness consumed her, unbidden tears filled her eyes. His response was automatic. He reached for her, and she went to him to cling in silent desperation. Their time together had been too short. A mere millisecond on the clock of eternity. It wasn't enough. She needed— wanted—more.

His arms surrounded her and she was lost in his strength as he gave in to the yearning to touch, to feel, to hold, and covered her mouth with his to drink of her in hopeless abandon. But the time for possession and quenched passion was past. To be merely together had to be enough, and reluctantly they drifted apart and out of the car.

He gestured to the café across the street and managed to smile, but hurt was near. He was about to feel the pain of loss again, for she was about to leave. "Maybe we can get you one last dish of ice cream." It was a stupid thing to say. As soon as the words were out, he wanted to take them back. There were too many other things that needed to be said. But her laughter took away the need to speak, and her unspoken understanding made it easy to pull her into his grasp and walk hip to hip and arm in arm into the diner that boasted huge hot-fudge sundaes.

He stopped to order two the moment they got past the door, and she kept her arms around him, her body against his, until she was forced to let go when he led her to a booth by the window. But she wasn't interested in what was happening outside. She gazed at him instead, not letting go of his hand even after they were seated next to each other. To let go meant possibly never being able to touch again. "What will you do when your government comes?"

"Don't worry about me."

"I must."

Her concern touched him. Her love moved him. He reached to brush his fingers over her cheek before cupping her head in his hand. It didn't seem possible that he was about to lose her, that someone was about to take her away—or that he was about to let it happen. Anger abruptly had him clenching his teeth, but the waitress appeared with her tray before he could sort through the bitter emotions. He released Kristiana and sat back. "Here's your ice cream."

But it seemed tasteless. The whipped cream, the chocolate, the smooth blend of vanilla didn't please Kristiana. Instead, it nearly choked her. She pushed her spoon through the melting mixture in front of her and looked up to find Derek watching her. Her heart jumped as their gazes locked, desire and frustration sizzling like a live wire between them, but she swallowed the yearnings and the empty hopes and pointed to his untouched sundae. "You are not hungry?"

"Not for food."

Her pulse jumped. "Derek . . ."

He shook his head to stop her from speaking and looked away to prevent her from seeing the helpless fury that was bubbling like bile in his throat. But his anger was quickly overcome by horror when he watched two cars fly into the visitors center parking lot on the other side of the street. As he watched, one squad car stopped beside the government vehicle he and Kristiana had just deserted.

"No!"

She followed his gaze and gasped, her stomach plummeting. "They have found us!"

"No," he denied. "It's not possible." But he was already standing as he watched Ron Rogers step out of one of the cars—followed by someone else he knew. "David!"

Kristiana recognized the men, too, but terror was closing her throat. All the running, the time spent trying to escape, had been for naught. She was trapped!

Not unaware of her thoughts and with his mind reeling, Derek found her hand and pulled her to her feet as he struggled to understand. David in Wyoming. How? Why? His appearing so soon after the phone call from the motel had to mean he'd left immediately on hanging up—and discovered Rogers and Magrini tied up in the motel room when he'd arrived. Derek nearly groaned out loud. Unwittingly his best friend had been Kristiana's and his undoing.

Silently cursing, Derek threw some bills onto the table and hurried Kristiana to a side door. By letting the agents go, David had allowed a bulletin to be put out on the stolen government sedan. It was a miracle they hadn't been stopped earlier. Yet that, Derek realized, was probably because of his lie. Rogers had thought they were going to Casper, not Sheridan.

"Kristiana, where should we go? Into the city or out of it? Will Roham be waiting outside?"

But she didn't hear him. Didn't see him. Instead, her heart pounding as she mindlessly clung to his hand, she could see only what she'd been fighting to avoid since the crash. Capture. Her nemesis was close. Roham was, too. Who would get to her first?

"Kristiana!"

Her head snapped back as Derek shook her by the shoulders, and she broke from the horror of morbid speculation to look up at him.

The fear in her eyes nearly had him pulling her to him, but a hug wouldn't insure her safety. "Where is Roham likely to be? Inside or outside the city?"

She shook her head in helpless response. Roham could already be on his way into the city, could be walking on a street toward them even as they spoke. "I do not know where he is now, but he would have waited, I think, outside the city."

"Then out we go." But what direction? Frowning, Derek pulled her from the café and the pursuers across the street, toward the opposite end of the block. They could be running away from the man they wanted to find, but they had no choice. The only safe place was out of the city.

Pulled into a race for the city limits, Kristiana didn't see the people who stared or hear the noises of traffic. She was conscious of only one thought as it kept going around and around in her mind. *Earth wasn't ready. Earth wasn't ready.* It echoed endlessly as she hurried blindly after Derek toward the growing darkness outside the town. She wanted to escape. Had to. Her eyes found his back. But she didn't want to leave her mate behind.

Unaware of her churning thoughts, Derek was consumed by emotions more bitter—and more savage—than hers. He was angrier than he could ever remember being. And fury mixed with despair had his blood and adrenaline pumping. He stopped at a street corner as the light turned red and gritted his teeth. Everyone—everything—was working against him. Even the traffic signals. There was a conspiracy to take Kristiana away from him. He pulled her into a run between darting cars but was jerked to a halt when she unexpectedly stumbled. Swinging to catch her, he pulled her into his arms. "Okay?"

She nodded, but her breathing was ragged and her limbs trembling. Just off a sickbed, she wasn't ready for an endurance race.

He swung to scour the streets for some kind of help—and found it in a taxi. "Let's go."

Falling inside with him, Kristiana looked up to see a middle-aged man wearing a red baseball cap and sporting a drooping mustache turn to smile at them. "Where to?"

Derek shoved a hundred-dollar bill into the driver's hands. "Outside the city. As fast as you can go."

The cabbie grinned and pocketed the bill. "Consider us gone."

It was a smooth run. No sirens, no flashing lights, very few cars. The only interference came from the radio dispatcher who kept up a nonstop flow of chatter that included messages about waiting fares, public announcements, and news bulletins. Only half listening to the empty talk coming from the speakers, Derek squeezed Kristiana's fingers. "We're going to make it," he whispered.

Clinging to his hand, she managed a smile. Terror and desire were ripping her heart apart. She had to choose between losing her freedom or losing her love. Her eyes clung in silent longing to his, and she was abruptly pulled against him and held with determined strength.

Her smell, her warmth, filled his senses, and he pressed his lips to the top of her head as she buried her face in his shoulder. He wanted to keep running, to keep her with him, but staying one jump ahead was becoming too difficult. Looking out the windshield, he saw an exit ahead. "Drive us up a mile from here, and you can drop us off."

"You got it." The driver met Derek's gaze in the rearview mirror. "But are you sure you want to be left out here? There's nothing around. No one."

"We'll be fine. We're meeting friends," Derek answered, and felt Kristiana tremble against him.

"Whatever you say," the cabbie agreed over the ongoing monologue of his company's dispatcher.

In a matter of moments he was gone, driving off and leaving them alone on the deserted country road. Derek could hear the taxi's cackling dispatcher continue to announce calls for service as the car sped back toward the freeway.

Taking a deep breath, he looked away from the departing cab and to the rapidly darkening countryside around them. "This should be deserted enough for Roham."

Following his gaze to the empty fields and rolling hills surrounding them, she nodded. "He will come now."

Derek swallowed. "Soon?"

It was impossible to answer. Not with her throat closing and her eyes misting. Throwing her arms around him, she could only feel, not speak, and he understood.

Folding her tightly against him, he simply held on as pain exploded in his chest. It was nearly over. Only minutes remained before she would be gone, and as the sun dipped toward the horizon and the shadows grew longer around them, she seemed to be trying to crawl inside him, even as he tried to absorb her.

Holding on, Kristiana was conscious only of Derek. His heartbeat beneath her ear, his arms keeping her near, the heat of his body warming hers, the unique male scent that was his, and the sense of completeness she felt only when he was with her. Together they were one. How would she ever be able to live without him? How had she ever thought she could? It had been foolish for her to believe loving and leaving him would be easy, that memories would be enough to last the lifetime she faced without him.

"I love you, Kristiana. I always will."

His words rumbled in his chest, and she tipped her head back to look up at him. It was impossible to make out his features completely in the growing darkness, but she didn't need to see to remember. "You will always be with me."

"And you with—" Derek stopped suddenly, listening. A thump in the distance. He held his breath for what he thought might be the end, but frowned when he realized no spaceship was making the noise he heard and suddenly recognized. "A helicopter!"

More than one. Without warning, they seemed to burst on the scene from every direction, flooding the field with light, catching him and Kristiana in their glare. Derek knew instantly what had happened. The taxi and its announcer. The driver had led the government agents right to them!

"No," he murmured, but before he could think or move, one chopper began dropping to the ground. "No!" But he was helpless to stop the invasion, to prevent the landing, to keep Ron Rogers and his men at bay as they jumped from the gyrating military machine.

"Derek . . ."

He looked down into fear-filled blue eyes, and the impotent fury in him nearly exploded at the sight. "Stay behind me," he ordered. "They don't have you yet."

Too frightened by the noise, too stunned by the relentless pursuit, and too tired to keep running, she didn't reply but merely slipped behind him to hide and to cling to him for what she was sure was the last time.

The escape she had hoped for was lost. Roham might be near, but he couldn't help her now. There would be no rescue. Her brother couldn't use weapons to free her. If he came, it would be too late, and he would be helpless to do more than watch as she was taken not only from the man she loved but from the life she knew.

Watching Rogers walk toward him, Derek gritted his teeth as he saw the signal that had the two hovering helicopters flying away to land behind the one already on the ground. Certain the man following Rogers was Magrini, Derek was prepared to issue a vile greeting, but he was shocked to find it was a friend instead. "David!"

"I didn't trust these guys to come after you alone," David told him, stepping around Rogers as the agent stopped a few feet from Derek.

Derek couldn't suppress his grin. David's declaration was fierce, his scowl at Rogers angry. "You shouldn't have come."

"You scared me. That goodbye sounded final."

Derek looked from friend to foe. "Let her go, Rogers. Let her go home. She's no threat to you, to us, to Earth." He reached back to pull Kristiana into the glaring light. "She's just a frightened woman."

"I can't do that."

"Can't? Or won't?" Derek demanded, pulling Kristiana close again.

"I told you, I've got a job to do."

Derek laughed. "Duty, honor, country. How many innocents have been hurt or killed because somebody was just doing his job? Following orders? You're not a robot, Rogers! Use your head instead of the rule book!"

Rogers remained silent.

"Her people are close. A few more minutes, and they will all be gone."

"It's too late," Rogers countered, gesturing to the helicopters behind him, the men watching with guns held ready. "I can't stop it. Neither can you. Turn her over."

Derek pushed Kristiana behind him again. "No way, Rogers. I'm not letting you take her."

"You can't stop us."

"No?" Derek pulled the small revolver he'd taken from Rogers at the motel from beneath his jacket. "I'll die before I let you touch her."

Chapter Seventeen

"Derek!" David's exclamation brought him a step closer, and from behind him, Kristiana gave a startled cry.

"Don't, David. Stay where you are." Derek's voice was deep and sure, his grip on the gun calm and steady. Rogers couldn't doubt his intent. The government agent froze, and so did everyone else behind him.

The field stilled as the two men faced each other, and only the crickets spoke as the last rays of sun disappeared, the only light remaining coming from the floodlights mounted on the war birds. But suddenly something else came to break the silence and to flash brightly over the meadow.

Swooping out of the blackness hiding the stars, the ship materialized directly above Kristiana and Derek in a blaze of light and sound.

Startled, Derek threw his head back to look up at the huge space vessel, his breath catching in shock and awe, but he grinned when he heard the alarmed cries of the men around him. Kristiana was safe! Pulling her into his arms again with a joyful whoop, he ignored David, who stood a few feet away, staring in openmouthed amazement, and Rogers and his armed men, who were all cringing, ducking and shouting in fear.

One of the soldiers fired a rifle, but the hostile action didn't have the desired effect. The ship didn't leave. Instead it retaliated with an unexpected blast of blinding light and an ear-piercing whine that was directed with military precision across the field. It encompassed all but Kristiana and Derek, and the result was immediate. Every member of the task force collapsed, and David Mallory went down with them.

Derek stared in disbelief as elation abruptly died. "David..." He barely felt Kristiana pull away from him as the ship started to move away to descend toward the field. He was aware only of his fallen friend.

"David," he repeated, the word a whisper, a prayer. Numb with shock, Derek hurried to the man who, still and silent, had been as close as a brother for more years than he could remember. He'd never considered the possibility that Kristiana's people would kill to save her....

"Your friend has not been harmed."

On one knee on the ground, Derek turned to look up at a tall, blond man, he would have recognized anywhere. Roham's smile was exactly like his sister's.

"I could not use the weapons, but our rules do not say anything of light and sound," Roham explained with an expressive shrug.

Laughing, Kristiana left her brother to fall to her knees beside Derek. "The pitch of the sound has made them unconscious. They will wake again shortly."

Relief whistled past Derek's lips on a sigh, and he tossed the gun he was still holding into the grass. "This is Roham?"

Her smile was his answer. It was brighter than any of
the lights illuminating the field.

He looked from her to the man standing over them.
"I was beginning to think I'd never meet you."

Roham held out a hand in the recognized Earth
greeting. "You have risked your life for my sister. I
thank you."

Accepting the handshake and rising, Derek grinned.
"She's worth it."

Following him to her feet as she continued to hold on
to his arm, Kristiana gestured to her brother. "Roham,
this is Derek Carpenter. He is a healer."

The pride in her voice nearly choked him, and Derek
felt hot color flood up his neck as he stammered a response. "I—I study medicine. My company makes it."

"An honored profession." Roham nodded but
turned to his sister. "We must go."

Derek's fingers immediately found hers, and she
turned toward him. Tears threatened to fall again, but
she forced them back with a smile. "I will never forget."

Blinded by grief himself, Derek found he couldn't
speak. He could only pull her to him for one final embrace.

"We must go," Roham repeated adamantly, frowning at the embrace his sister was receiving from an
Earthling.

It took more strength than Derek knew he possessed
to let her slide out of his arms, and more courage than
she could muster to take the first step away. Roham had
to take her hand to force her feet to move, but her eyes
clung to Derek's. She didn't want to let him go.

Watching the distance separating them grow, Derek's fingers clenched into impotent fists. She was walking out of his life!

Steadily moving away, her face lined with tears, Kristiana held his gaze for as long as she could, turning away only at the last moment. The movement broke the invisible cord that still held the two of them together—and snapped Derek's control. He jumped after her.

"No!"

Roham stopped in alarm at the angry tone, and Kristiana spun in surprise.

"You can't go! Not alone." Suddenly sure of what he wanted to do, of what he had to do, Derek strode forward to take her hand from her brother's before meeting Roham's hard stare with one of his own. "Kristiana's my mate."

Roham's eyes widened, and he swung to look at his sister. "This is true?"

She nodded without hesitation and moved closer to Derek. "He is my life mate by my choice."

Roham's frown was ferocious. The implications of her declaration were far-reaching. "But Earth..."

"Is not ready?" Derek finished, his fingers tightening on hers. "Maybe not. But I am." He turned to Kristiana and grasped her by the shoulders. "I want to come with you. I can help your people. You know I can, and I want to."

Her smile and knees trembled, and her heart quaked with the possibility. "You are certain?"

Derek nodded, and a smile spread across his face. "More certain than I have ever been of anything before." Looking into her glowing eyes, he knew. This chance to help a people was what he'd somehow been working and preparing for his entire life. He could help them. It was his destiny. And so was she. It was Kristiana he'd been waiting for, and she would lead him to, and share with him, the task he needed to do.

She laughed and threw her arms around him. "We will find a way, won't we, Roham?"

When she turned to her brother, he was still frowning, but Roham had never been able to resist her wishes. Not since the day she was born. "The council will not be happy," he murmured, scowling at Derek. "And you may never be able to return."

The warning brought no fear. Derek merely hugged Kristiana and nodded. "I know."

Roham looked from Derek to his sister. The love was there, shining between them. He would not be the one to separate them or to break that precious bond, no matter what the consequences. And there would be consequences. He nodded. "Then we all go. Together."

Kristiana leapt from Derek to throw her arms around the man who could be her twin. "Thank you, Roham."

He winced. "Thank the council when we get back."

She laughed at his rueful grimace. The council would not be happy, but she didn't care. Her heart singing, she swung back to hold a hand out to Derek. "We must go."

He grasped her fingers, ready and willing, but gestured to the man still lying behind him. "I need to say goodbye to David."

Her smile of understanding warmed him to the bone. He was making the right choice. She squeezed his fingers quickly before turning to her brother. "We will wait over here."

Roham rolled his eyes as she led him away. "You cause me great trouble."

"You like trouble."

His grin returned as they walked away from Derek, but his glance backward was curious—and protective. "He is a good mate?"

"As good as you will be. And he will help our people." She smiled and turned to watch Derek kneel next to his friend.

"David?"

David groaned as his shoulder was shaken, but, blinking, managed to raise his head. "What happened?"

"You were stunned." Derek helped him sit up. "But listen, I don't have much time."

"Much time. What...?"

"I'm going with her."

David gasped, the past and the present colliding abruptly as he spotted the spaceship and the two people standing not far from it. He recognized them both and struggled to his feet. "Kristiana and Roham. But..."

"It's what I want, David. I've been waiting—working for it—for her, forever. She's what's been missing in my life, and she'll help me reach that goal I've always been searching for."

"But..." Arguments came but evaporated before they hit his lips, extinguished by the light in his friend's eyes. David took Derek's hand in a firm grip. Questions pounded through his brain, but only one broke through. "Will you come back?"

Derek shrugged and grinned. "I don't know. But I told you I'd let you know what happened, no matter what, and I will. Somehow."

David laughed and abruptly pulled Derek to him for a bear hug. "You'll be missed."

Derek nodded, emotion tightening his throat, even though he had no regrets, and he backed away. "Take care of the company. It's yours now." He handed David his wallet. "And see about taking care of the owner of the Pontiac Firebird I borrowed, will you? The feds will explain."

David laughed in disbelief. "Will do," he promised. His laughter died as he stared into his friend's eyes. "You take care of yourself—and her." Derek nodded, and David watched him back away. Doubts and fear for Derek's safety and happiness made David frown, but the moment he saw Derek step into Kristiana's waiting arms, his frown disappeared. They belonged together. "Have a good flight!"

Derek laughed at the call and waved, but he didn't let go of Kristiana. He kept her firmly by his side as they moved as one to follow Roham up the ramp and into the craft.

They were going home.

Epilogue

Derek stared out the window at the stars sprinkled across the black velvet of space. He was still having a hard time believing he was really in a ship taking him to another planet.

A grin spread across his mouth as he leaned against the bulkhead to admire the view he was sure he'd never tire of. Roham had given him a tour of the craft shortly after they'd gotten under way. The vessel wasn't as large as the USS *Enterprise* Derek was used to seeing on television, but it was easily as impressive. And it was real.

The whole idea was almost overwhelming. Almost, because Kristiana kept him rooted in reality. As he had been her guide in a strange new world, so now was she his, and looking out for his best interests had led her to convince her brother to make a stop on the way back to Takyam. In Chicago.

Derek's grin grew. He didn't think Roham was very good at saying no to Kristiana, a dilemma he could well understand, but while he hadn't thought of it, Derek was glad she'd had the foresight to allow him to visit his old home one more time before going on to his new one. It had given him the chance to say goodbye and to gather those few things that he wanted to take from one life into another.

He shook his head in silent amazement. He'd found precious little in the way of personal mementos to bring onto the ship. Some photo albums, a couple of sentimental trinkets, clothes. But the bulk of what he'd wanted to bring along had been books—about medicine, about plants, about technology that cured. And Kristiana had insisted on packing up the aloe plant.

Roham had grumbled about the stop and the extra cargo, but his actions had spoken louder than his words. His eyes had lit up at the books and their possibilities, but he'd also taken the time to look out for his sister's mate.

Derek sighed. Maybe it was natural the universe over for one independent male to recognize another. Roham had realized it would be important for Derek not to be totally dependent on Kristiana for every necessity and had suggested taking items from the house that would be of more worth off the planet than on. Selling or trading them would give Derek useful currency and free him to pursue his determination to help Takyam's people.

His medical school experience left Derek under no illusions. He wasn't infallible, and he wasn't going to save a world. He, as one man, was only going to help. Kristiana had said her people needed someone to show them the way, and he believed he could be that someone, could put them on the right track. It would be up to others, both doctors and scientists, to do the rest. Still, he could get them started, and it was a challenge he was looking forward to—and one that would keep him busy for a lifetime.

He sighed happily. No regrets. No looking back. He was only interested in what lay ahead. But he was distracted from his contemplation of the future by a pair of slender arms that unexpectedly slid around his waist.

"You are happy?"

Derek turned in the embrace to cup Kristiana's face in his hands. She was worried for him. It was reflected in her eyes and her words. "Absolutely."

She clung to him as his lips covered hers. It was still hard for her to believe that he was with her. She hadn't lost him. He hadn't been left behind. Her mate had sacrificed everything to be with her—even though he kept telling her that it had been no sacrifice at all. The kiss ended, and she snuggled against him. "Your sigh was quite heavy."

He grunted. "Probably because I was thinking about the council."

She grinned. Her mate and the council were bound to be seeing a lot of each other, for it was the council that determined what was spent for what cause on the planet. The people had been clamoring for more funds for medical research. She had little doubt Derek would be the one to convince the council to do as the people wished. He was a determined man. "I am glad it was them and not me making you sigh so."

"You make me sigh, too," he assured her as he slowly began to pull her toward the bed across their cabin.

She didn't resist the gentle tug of his hands. Already he was adapting, learning, and his eagerness proved to her that he wasn't sorry he'd made the decision to stay with her. The closer to Takyam they got, the more excited he became—and the more plans he told her about.

She fell with him onto the bed. The council was definitely going to have a hard time saying no to her mate....

"How long did you say it would be before we reached Takyam?"

She trembled as he nibbled at her throat, her ears, and kissed her eyes. "In Earth time..."

His head came up, and he fell back onto the pillows beside her with another sigh. "I suppose this means I'm going to have to learn basic things like telling time all over again. It'll be like going back to school." But he didn't sound disappointed. He sounded eager.

She sat up to smile down at him. "I will be your teacher."

His smile echoed hers as he grabbed a fistful of her long hair. Yes, she would show him the stars, whole new worlds, and guide him into a new culture, and he'd follow her gladly. Because no matter what planet he was on, he belonged only to and with her. "I think this Earthling can still teach you a thing or two, too."

She squealed as he abruptly grabbed her and rolled to pin her beneath him on the bed. Her fingers linked behind his head as he hovered above her. He was her mate, her life. Where he was, so was her home. "I cannot wait for you to demonstrate."

He grinned and lowered his head toward hers. "Then let the lessons begin."

HARLEQUIN®

A M E R I C A N ◆ R O M A N C E®

Their idea of a long night is a sexy woman and a warm bed—not a squalling infant!

To them, a "bottle" means champagne—not formula!

But Matt Hale and Ben Cooper are about to get a rude awakening. They're about to become

ACCIDENTAL DADS

Join us next month for a very special duet, as Matt and Ben take the plunge into fatherhood.

Don't miss

#607 DADDY CHRISTMAS by Cathy Gillen Thacker

and

#608 MOMMY HEIRESS by Linda Randall Wisdom
Available November 1995

You've never seen daddies like these before!

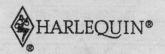

Harlequin Romance ®

AVAILABLE IN OCTOBER—A BRAND-NEW COVER DESIGN FOR HARLEQUIN ROMANCE

Harlequin Romance has a fresh new eye-catching cover.

We're bringing you an exciting new cover design, but Harlequin Romance is still committed to bringing you warm and contemporary love stories that are sure to touch your heart!

See how we've changed and look for these fabulous stories with a brand-new look:

#3379 **Brides for Brothers**
  by Debbie Macomber
#3380 **The Best Man**
  by Shannon Waverly
#3381 **Once Burned**
  by Margaret Way
#3382 **Legally Binding**
  by Jessica Hart

Available in October, wherever Harlequin books are sold.

Harlequin Romance ®—
Dare To Dream

HRNEW

OFFICIAL RULES

PRIZE SURPRISE SWEEPSTAKES 3448

NO PURCHASE OR OBLIGATION NECESSARY

Three Harlequin Reader Service 1995 shipments will contain respectively, coupons for entry into three different prize drawings, one for a Panasonic 31" wide-screen TV, another for a 5-piece Wedgwood china service for eight and the third for a Sharp ViewCam camcorder. To enter any drawing using an Entry Coupon, simply complete and mail according to directions.

There is no obligation to continue using the Reader Service to enter and be eligible for any prize drawing. You may also enter any drawing by hand printing the words "Prize Surprise," your name and address on a 3"x5" card and the name of the prize you wish that entry to be considered for (i.e., Panasonic wide-screen TV, Wedgwood china or Sharp ViewCam). Send your 3"x5" entries via first-class mail (limit: one per envelope) to: Prize Surprise Sweepstakes 3448, c/o the prize you wish that entry to be considered for, P.O. Box 1315, Buffalo, NY 14269-1315, USA or P.O. Box 610, Fort Erie, Ontario L2A 5X3, Canada.

To be eligible for the Panasonic wide-screen TV, entries must be received by 6/30/95; for the Wedgwood china, 8/30/95; and for the Sharp ViewCam, 10/30/95.

Winners will be determined in random drawings conducted under the supervision of D.L. Blair, Inc., an independent judging organization whose decisions are final, from among all eligible entries received for that drawing. Approximate prize values are as follows: Panasonic wide-screen TV ($1,800); Wedgwood china ($840) and Sharp ViewCam ($2,000). Sweepstakes open to residents of the U.S. (except Puerto Rico) and Canada, 18 years of age or older. Employees and immediate family members of Harlequin Enterprises, Ltd., D.L. Blair, Inc., their affiliates, subsidiaries and all other agencies, entities and persons connected with the use, marketing or conduct of this sweepstakes are not eligible. Odds of winning a prize are dependent upon the number of eligible entries received for that drawing. Prize drawing and winner notification for each drawing will occur no later than 15 days after deadline for entry eligibility for that drawing. Limit: one prize to an individual, family or organization. All applicable laws and regulations apply. Sweepstakes offer void wherever prohibited by law. Any litigation within the province of Quebec respecting the conduct and awarding of the prizes in this sweepstakes must be submitted to the Regies des loteries et Courses du Quebec. In order to win a prize, residents of Canada will be required to correctly answer a time-limited arithmetical skill-testing question. Value of prizes are in U.S. currency.

Winners will be obligated to sign and return an Affidavit of Eligibility within 30 days of notification. In the event of noncompliance within this time period, prize may not be awarded. If any prize or prize notification is returned as undeliverable, that prize will not be awarded. By acceptance of a prize, winner consents to use of his/her name, photograph or other likeness for purposes of advertising, trade and promotion on behalf of Harlequin Enterprises, Ltd., without further compensation, unless prohibited by law.

For the names of prizewinners (available after 12/31/95), send a self-addressed, stamped envelope to: Prize Surprise Sweepstakes 3448 Winners, P.O. Box 4200, Blair, NE 68009.

RPZ KAL